Scott Killian and the Letter (second edition)
Copyright (c) 2024,2026 by Jessica Manges

All rights reserved. No part of this book may be reproduced in any form or by any means.

Published by Acorn Ridge Publishing
ISBN second edition 979-8-9950636-0-5

This book and all characters in it are a work of fiction. Real locations that are mentioned are used fictitiously. While the narrative is set in the future, it is a work of speculative imagination and is not intended as a prediction or forecast of actual events to come. Any resemblance to future persons, living or dead, or actual events is purely coincidental.

First Edition: 2024
Second Edition: 2026

Global One News

Gabriel Friedman announces no extensions for mandatory chip despite pushback from men in Jerusalem.

Press Release Date May 29th

Charlene Novak – Global Press Association

The Department of Homeland Security is urging residents of the US to register for the required chip over the next couple of days. While pushback from the two men in Jerusalem, whom some people are calling witnesses, has been made, Friedman insists that these two men are terrorists and demands an immediate cease and desist.

"The TSA has already prohibited passengers from boarding airline transportation," said Secretary of Homeland Security Lillian Paige. "We back Gabriel Friedman on this and insist that no public transportation will be accessible without the chip by the end of this week. This is simply an upgrade to the REAL ID Act and is required by law, and residents have had ample time to be compliant."

<u>Chapter One</u>

I walked with my head down, trying to remain inconspicuous and gazing upon the many weeds poking their way through the cracks of the fragmented sidewalk. Keeping my head down, I peeked up as I turned left onto the next street. The shady figure loomed at the corner of the bus station, seeming to study my every move.

I used to be frightened when I'd see him hovering about. Over time, my fear had changed to more of an uneasy curiosity. My parents, Samantha and Doug Killian, had disappeared a little over three years ago. Not long after they'd gone, I'd started noticing this man watching and following me. Lately, his presence seemed more frequent and obvious.

I could feel his unnerving gaze even through his pair of dark sunglasses, which he always wore alongside an Indianapolis Colts baseball cap and a long dark coat over layered clothing. He stood around six feet tall, had an average build, and was Caucasian. He always stood just far enough away for me to be unable to make out any specific facial features or other physical attributes, and he always vanished as quickly as he appeared. I felt helpless knowing he was probably stalking me from afar. Sometimes I thought I was being paranoid; however, my instincts told me my frequent sightings of the man couldn't be coincidences. I wanted to convince myself it was possible he just lived in the area near the bus station, but my feeling of apprehension and my inclination for survival fought my ability to be convinced.

I sat inside the graffiti-covered bus shelter watching the litter on the streets blow by as I waited to head home from school for the last time. I didn't carry a bookbag or many personal items, as they would most likely get stolen on the unscrupulous streets.

I took public transport instead of riding the school bus. Not only did I get home faster, but three years ago, my school bus driver, who had been accustomed to seeing my mom greet me each day, had asked where my mom was one afternoon after she had disappeared. I'd lied and told the bus driver my mom was at a dentist's appointment. I'd never ridden the school bus again, fearing people would notice I was alone and would make a report. Not having to ride the bus with a bunch of freshmen and sophomores had been an added benefit.

Today was the last day of my senior year. It was a warm Wednesday afternoon in Franklin, Indiana, but I still kept up my hood to obscure my face as much as possible from the vast array of facial-recognition screens around me. The bus stop was a six-by-six-foot box full of screens that played advertisements for items directed at the individual scanned. Some people were scanned before the screens could capture their faces because of the RFFC chips they'd had implanted in either their hands or foreheads.

RFFC stood for Radio Frequency Field Communication. They combined the technologies of RFID and NFC. I hadn't gotten the chip yet and frankly wasn't too keen on the fact that they were going to become mandatory. Even when my parents had been around, I'd liked my privacy. I would come home from school and head straight to my room, shut the door, put in my earbuds, and play video games until I was forced to come down for dinner. I was sure that I hadn't acted any differently than most fifteen-year-old boys, but I regretted how little time I'd spent with my parents when I'd had the chance. Now that I was eighteen, graduated, and alone, I was warming up to the idea of having my friends around all the time.

The ads on the bus shelter started to change.

"Do you have what it takes to lead people into the future? Join the One World governance today, and see how you can make a difference!"

This ad usually only played for people with RFFC chips. It must have picked up on someone walking by or maybe the stranger who always seemed to be watching me. The ad gave me the creeps. It featured either a lady with a permanent joker smile on her face or a young guy that looked like he had never blinked a day in his life. Luckily, I was saved by the bus, which pulled up to the terminal before the ad could finish.

Most people could walk right onto the bus using their RFFC chips, but I still had an old-fashioned bus pass. Each passenger had to pause on the step until the blue light that encased the entrance turned green. Each bus had a UVC-Sterilization entrance that supposedly helped reduce the spread of viruses on public transit. These entrances were on most public doorways and were mandatory in all government buildings.

Disease had been one of the largest causes of death up until recently. In a shorter time span, contaminated water had become the leading cause, resulting in the deaths of thousands if not millions of people. The authorities said they'd tested many locations. An unknown poison had polluted thousands of square miles of rivers and springs. Everywhere you went, there were precautions in place against both these causes of death.

Gary, the usual driver, scanned my bus pass. Gary was a super friendly middle-aged Black man that wore an animated smile every time I saw him. Besides my close friends, he was one of the few people I talked to.

"Good afternoon, Mr. Scott! How was my favorite passenger's last day of school?"

"Hey, Gary, pretty much the same as always."

"That good, huh?" Gary replied. "I have to say, I sure will miss seeing you every morning and afternoon."

"Oh, ha, well, don't worry, you'll still see me all the time. I don't plan on moving or getting my license any time soon. In fact, I need to start looking for a job."

"Oh, boy, I guess if you ever need a reference, I can tell them you always show up to the bus stop on time."

We both chuckled, then Gary handed back my card, and I headed to one of the front seats. The ride was free, but everyone had to be scanned so they could keep track of each person that walked on or off the bus.

In front of my seat was another screen, which started playing an advertisement for the newest Converse. I had on an old pair that I typically wore with old jeans and a hooded sweatshirt. How the screen knew what I wore was something I'd stopped questioning about a year ago, a few months after I'd started noticing how personal all the ads had become. My mom had always joked about how she'd thought her phone was spying on her since it would pop up related ads every time she mentioned she needed to get something from the store. My current reality was a huge escalation from that.

The bus stopped at the terminal closest to my house. "Be safe, Mr. Scott, and hope you have a great summer!" There was a twinge of sadness in

Gary's voice, as though he was going to miss me. I offered him a fist bump before I headed off the bus.

I could hear the advertisements for the new mandated chips playing as I walked past the terminal toward my street. I would need to get one to get a job; by the time I found a place to work, the chips would be mandatory for employment and to ride the bus, too. I tried not to think too much about it because it stressed me out. I was great at pushing things aside that made me feel under pressure, and even my teachers had loved pointing out my procrastination techniques. Forgetting a problem existed was my only coping mechanism.

The noise from the terminal ads faded, as I continued walking down the cracked sidewalk. It was a nice day out, which was rare these days. There'd been severe droughts until about two months ago, when a continuous torrential downpour had begun. My neighborhood was in a suburban area about thirty-five minutes south of downtown Indianapolis. It was an older community, with lots of trees and privacy fences. Some of the houses had been boarded up, and some had been broken into by squatters or thieves.

As I walked down the sidewalk, I thought I saw a shadowy figure out of the corner of my eye, but when I jerked my head around, no one was there except Mrs. Mulligan across the street watering her lawn. I could swear she was watering her lawn every time I passed by her. With all the rain we had been getting, I was surprised her yard hadn't flooded.

I turned back around and could see Inspector Bucket heading in my direction. Because so many people had disappeared in my town, there were numerous stray dogs and cats around the neighborhood. Many of the shelters had shut down due to lack of funding. I carried dog treats in my pocket, and Inspector Bucket, whose name was engraved on the tag on his red collar, knew this all too well. His name was from a Charles Dickens book, I'd found after Googling it, and I imagined Inspector Bucket's former owners must have been huge fans of the author. I'd tried to get ahold of his owners the first time I'd come across Bucket, but no one had answered when I'd knocked at the house of the yard he'd been in, and the house had eventually been boarded up like so many others.

Bucket had the white markings of a border collie, but the rest of his fur was golden instead of black. His coat was soft and long. A lot of people helped take care of the abandoned pets in the area, including Bucket, but I believed I was his favorite.

I pet him for a while, and after giving him a few more treats, Bucket ran toward Mrs. Mulligan's, in all likelihood to get a drink of water from her ever-flowing garden hose. I ran down the street, passing five more houses before arriving at mine. Before I walked in, I looked around to see if anyone was watching me.

When I walked in, the motion detector went off, and my virtual personal assistant popped up on the television screen.

"Good afternoon, Scott. Congratulations on your last day of school. Is there anything I can help you with today?" Her voice was monotone and soothing. Her face had been designed by my dad when he'd installed the cameras and security system in the house. Most avatars I had seen looked realistic, and she was no exception. She had brown hair and soft brown eyes that resembled my mother's. My dad had frequently brought home different devices his company was working on for us to try.

"Pat, play some music, and set the house to seventy degrees." My dad had called her Pat because the system had come in a box marked "Personal Assistant Technology." Big band music from the 1940s filled the house. The genre was my mother's favorite, and it'd grown on me until I'd learned to love it as much as she did. I sang along out loud. My voice was so bad I was sure even Pat took offense.

The house still felt lonely even with Pat and the music playing throughout. It was an old Queen-Anne-style two-story home that my grandfather had bought when my dad had been a teenager. The house had been remodeled a few years before my parents had disappeared, so the interior was modern looking. The dungeon-like basement had been turned into a movie room, and the kitchen had the latest gadgets from my dad's company.

My grandfather had liked to work on houses, remodeling them and flipping them in the area. Most of the memories I had with my grandfather included tools. I'd loved helping him hammer in nails when I was younger and eventually had helped him design and build furniture until the day he'd passed.

My mom, like my grandfather, was a very kind and intelligent woman. My dad's parents had seemed closer to my mom than they had been to my dad. They'd gone to the same church where my mom had worked as the administrative assistant. My mom and grandparents had also liked to prepare for whatever scenario one could imagine. My mom would spend time canning with my grandma while I'd worked outside in the shed with my grandpa.

My parents were very frugal, which turned out to be in my favor. I had been living off the things my mom had been storing since I was a baby. My dad had made good money as owner and CEO at Killian Tech Innovations, KTI for short. His company was one of the many that had joined a massive global conglomerate to push technological advances and innovations like UVC-Sterilization entrances.

Since we lived way below our means, my parents had saved a lot of money, which still paid for the house utilities. The bills had been set up on autopay, so I'd never had any issues with cancelations or anything getting shut off. I even still received a monthly subscription to *Reader's Digest* in the mail.

I'd never reported my parents as missing. A few million people had disappeared simultaneously on a devastating day over three years ago. Everyone had either lost someone they knew or known someone who had. Kids with missing parents were told to report it in school, but any student who did ended up going away, probably into some foster care system. I wasn't about to live with strangers.

I had been living by myself since I was fifteen. I knew the money wouldn't last forever; I wasn't sure how much was in the account to begin with. I had my mom's debit card, but since I didn't know her PIN, I just used it as a credit card and didn't know how to check the balance. I tried to use it only for things I absolutely needed, plus a few extras here and there.

Pretty soon, without the chip, my mom's card and my parents' bank account would be obsolete, too. To get the chip, I would have to go to the local Global One or social security office and pledge my allegiance to the Global One leader, who was also the secretary general of the United World Federation. All my money and assets would be transferred over to a blockchain bank account called the Babylonian Exchange, the new One World currency.

The new chip would take the place of everything: debit or credit cards, insurance cards, IDs, you name it. Vendors would simply scan the chip in their consumers' hands or foreheads to charge all their purchases to their Global One blockchain account.

In the kitchen at the back of the house, I poured myself a glass of Coke, one of the "extras" I afforded myself. I wasn't ready to give up drinking soda just yet, and Coke was one of the few sodas still available in stores. As I walked back toward the front of the house, I felt the Coke in my hand sloshing all over me. The timbers in the ceiling groaned. Another earthquake.

Earthquakes had been more frequent recently in Indiana and surrounding states because of the fault lines. At least, that was what they kept saying on the news.

The beams continued to creak as the house began to settle.

BOOM. BOOM. BOOM.

The remainder of my Coke splashed up on my face, and my heart jumped into my throat. I spun toward the front door and saw my friends Carl and Max pounding on it.

"Someone is at the front door," Pat informed me.

"You think?" I often replied to Pat with sarcasm though her responses were always literal.

"Yes, someone is at the front door."

I opened the door with a stern look on my face to see Carl and Max standing on the porch laughing. "Geez, Carl, you made me lose my drink."

"That was hilarious!" Carl said, still laughing. "I wasn't even trying to scare you that time, but that was awesome!"

I punched him in the arm. "You owe me a Coke, punk."

"I guess that makes five Cokes I owe you this week then," Carl laughed. "Did you feel that last quake? I swear they are getting worse. Especially if they are going to make you lose your entire drink."

"Pat, turn down the music," I said, walking back into the house and leaving the door open behind me for Carl and Max to enter. I grabbed a dish towel and stood in front of the mirror hanging in our living room to wipe down my gray sweatshirt, which wasn't so forgiving of the Coke splatter. My brown hair swooped down across my blue eyes enough that they were barely visible.

"So how do you guys feel now that you are grown men like me? Ha, I mean, high school graduates, that is," Max asked, grinning.

"Well, I guess I should have figured out what I should be doing next. I was so focused on getting through this part of my life without my parents, I didn't plan very well for what I would do after high school." I laughed a little, but it was nervous laughter. I was nervous about my future though I was glad my friends supported me through everything.

"I would still like to go to the police academy, but I still need to wait a few years for that. In the meantime, my aunt has some work for me to do to help her with her business. She said I can help her with pickup and deliveries and stuff," Carl said. His aunt was a seamstress, but she seemed to have a lot of side gigs as well.

"It looks like I may be getting a promotion at work soon," Max said. "I haven't gotten anything official, so I wasn't going to say anything, but the boss asked me if I would be interested the other day, and I was like, heck yeah!"

"That's awesome Max. I know you've liked working at the shop," I replied. "Maybe I can come by with you to see if there are any openings that I qualify for. Just put in a good word for me, will you?"

"Oh, I'm sure there is something they can find for you to do," Max said. "I am always behind on my appointments because I have to clean up, find the tools I need for the next job, or file some paperwork. I know for a fact some of the other guys are behind just like me, and we could definitely use a hand and even teach you a few things while you are helping us out."

"Sounds great," I replied.

"Anyway, Sam said his parents are cool if we want to head over there and have dinner with them," Carl cut in. Carl rarely stopped thinking about food.

"I know I'm in. Anything beats my mom's cooking," Max added.

Carl made his way into the kitchen and rummaged through the cabinets. He pulled out a bag of chips and started eating them a handful at a time.

"Didn't you just say that we could head over to Sam's to eat?" I asked, shaking my head.

"Dude, it's called an appetizer. Plus, I need it for energy to walk to the bus stop," Carl replied.

"It's not like you didn't just eat a candy bar on the way over here either or anything," Max said sarcastically.

"It's a good thing Sam invited us over for dinner so you don't eat your poor aunt out of her house," I snickered.

Sam Stern, Max Lambert, and Carl Williamson were my only friends. Carl and I met in elementary school when we'd been in the same class and ridden the same bus. We'd started hanging out in third grade, when I was being picked on by some bullies on the playground. Carl had made it a point to let the kids know I was under his protection, not that I'd understood what that meant at the time, but the kids had stopped teasing me, and Carl and I had become inseparable.

Carl and I met Sam during our freshman year, and the three of us had been inseparable ever since, even more so after the disappearances. It was one of the things that Carl and I had in common. Carl's dad had passed away when he was eight, so when his mom had disappeared, he'd moved in with his aunt Aniyah who lived just a little under a mile from my house. Carl had vowed to become a detective after his mom had gone to find not only her but the others that had disappeared at the same time. He was sure there was a connection between all of the disappearances despite the media's insistence that they'd been isolated instances. Even the detective on his mom's case seemed to think there was no hope.

Carl was six foot five, Black, and very neat although some of his pants didn't seem long enough. He'd grown about three inches our senior year, and his aunt was having a hard time keeping up with him. He'd already outgrown his Christmas clothes, and he could just forget about wearing anything he'd bought at the beginning of the school year. Luckily, his aunt had bought some of his pants a couple sizes longer and hemmed them so she could take out the hems as needed. Carl loved playing practical jokes and making stupid puns. He often made light of tough situations, which was honestly what I'd needed to keep myself going these past few years.

Sam was closer to my six-foot frame, and his hair was a shade of brown darker than mine. He kept it shorter on the sides and longer on the top, and he often sported a little facial hair. Sam's family had moved back here from Israel a couple of years before the peace treaty in Israel had been signed. Before that, they'd lived in New York. Sam liked living in the States, enjoyed his Jewish culture, and frequently threw out Hebrew words that we'd all grown accustomed to. The Stern family often had all of us over for dinner. Sam was very intelligent and more serious than Carl but still loved Carl's practical jokes and was easily swayed by Carl to go along with them. I relied on Sam to help me with any classes I struggled with.

We'd met Max about three years ago. He had graduated a year before us and lived on my street with his parents. He was the only blonde in the group though he always covered his hair with a Reds baseball cap, and he stood about two inches shorter than Sam and me. He rode his skateboard everywhere he went and had been a bit of a loner until I'd met him. I'd literally run into him about a year ago when, after getting off the bus, I'd knocked him off his skateboard. We'd been close friends ever since. It had taken me a lot longer to confide in Max about my parents, but he'd always confided in me and had dealt with a lot of pain after his older sister had been killed on the same day my parents had disappeared. Max didn't like to get too serious when we talked. He didn't have Carl's cheesy sense of humor, either. He mostly liked video games and skateboarding.

Carl's aunt and Sam's parents were the only ones outside of my friends that knew my parents were missing. Most of my mom's friends were missing, too, so no one ever reached out to her, and my dad's only friend had been his work. One day, a man named Steven Whittaker had called me and asked if my dad was home, and I'd told him that he was traveling for business, which he used to do a lot. The man gave me his number and said he ran the company when my dad was traveling and hadn't heard from him and to call him if I ever needed anything. That had been the last time I'd heard from anyone at my dad's company.

"I would love to head over there for dinner as soon as possible so Carl doesn't eat all my snacks. I'm pretty psyched I won't have to scrounge for food again, plus Sam's mom is the best cook ever," I added.

Food was getting harder and harder to come by. First, there'd been a wheat shortage, then it'd been sugar. Canned food could only be found sporadically, and if there was food to be bought, affording a monthly grocery list essentially required one to take out a mortgage. Most of the food I had in the house was canned or whatever I could find on the shelves of the frozen food aisle. Eating a home-cooked meal was so much better than eating SpaghettiOs straight from the can like I usually did.

Chapter Two

The three of us headed out the door toward the bus stop. "Pat, run the vacuum," I said before closing the door behind me.

Mrs. Mulligan's plump frame was in view as soon as we hit the sidewalk. She was still watering her manicured lawn. The neighbors had gotten annoyed with how much water she had used for her lawn during the droughts, but that hadn't stopped her. I wasn't sure how there wasn't a river flowing down the street from her house. There were, however, fresh dog prints going down the sidewalk, no doubt from Inspector Bucket. I'd refilled my pockets with more dog treats before we'd left the house in case we ran into him again on the way out.

"You still feeding that dog that runs around here?" Max asked, seeing the prints.

"Ha, yeah, I don't really feed him, I just give him some treats. If he comes by the house looking hungry, I have some dog food saved for him," I replied. "Inspector Bucket is a neighborhood favorite, so I think that boy is well-fed."

"That's what we are. Just a bunch of strays heading over to Sam's house so Mrs. S can feed us well," Carl added.

We all walked onto the bus and scanned our cards. Gary's shift was over, so there was a different driver I had never seen before. When we sat down, the bus started playing ads for Coke as if it had sensed I had some spilled over my sweatshirt.

We exited the bus at the station closest to Sam's house. That was when I noticed the man in the Colts hat sitting on the bench across the street. He was looking toward us, fidgeting with a pen in his hand.

"Have either of you guys seen that man before?" I asked.

Max shrugged and shook his head no, but Carl squinted toward the man. "Uh, I mean, maybe if I got a better look at his face, but I think I've seen him around before. Don't think I've ever seen him with anybody. I'll go up to him right now and ask him his name if you want."

"No! I know you would, but don't," I said. "I see him a lot, sometimes multiple times a day, like he has been following me around. It's kind of weird, but it's been going on for a couple of years. I thought it was just a coincidence, but lately, I feel like I've been seeing him more, and it doesn't just feel like a coincidence anymore."

"Well, maybe we should get Inspector Bucket on the case," Carl snickered.

"Think about it," Max said. "If you've seen this guy around for a couple of years and he has never approached you and nothing bad has happened, then I'm pretty sure he probably just goes to some of the same places or areas you go to. He hasn't tried anything, so I doubt he is anybody important. I wouldn't worry about it. He seems way more harmless than most of the punks around here that will steal from anyone anytime they see food."

Max continued to walk ahead, but Carl straggled behind and kept glancing back at the man on the bench until we were too far away to make him out.

When we arrived at Sam's house, the smell of brisket was all I could focus on even before we walked into the house. It was an old Italianate-style home with lots of character, stylish corbels, and rounded windows on the white-painted brick front. The porch had four pillars and wrapped around the front door in a semi-circle. An arc trellis covered in grape leaves started around the side of the house and led to the back, where they kept chickens and goats. More and more people were starting to grow their own food. Sam's mom, Mila, had given me some seeds to start my own garden. The only thing that ever came up in my yard was zucchini, which I hated, so it just looked like a big mess of weeds.

"Shalom! Come in, come in! You boys must be famished," Mila greeted us at the door.

Max walked in with a half-smile on his face. Carl gave Mila a big hug, lifting her off the floor, and with her small frame, she looked swallowed up by him.

"Hello, Mrs. Stern," I said after Carl had released her and headed to the dinner table. "Thank you for having us over."

"Scott, you know you can call me Mila. Dinner is ready on the table. You boys should head on in."

Sam pointed at the Coke stains on my shirt. "You're a bit of a schlemiel, you know that?"

Sam joined his older brother Nate and their dad sitting at the table. Sam and Nate were night-and-day different in terms of style but could pass for twins if they wanted to. Nate wore a white linen Coofandy shirt with a silver wristwatch, had styled hair, was clean-shaven, and wore contacts. Sam wore a t-shirt that read *I try to tell chemistry jokes but there is no reaction* across the chest. His hair was sticking up in an intentionally messy way, and he wore black-rimmed glasses and a matching smartwatch.

Sam and Nate were relentlessly elbowing each other, which made Mila give them a look only moms could give. Sam sat up straight, but Nate punched him under the table. Mila was small, but her words made the boys stop everything they were doing. "If I see one more elbow or fist at the table, the most you boys will be eating is goat food."

"All right, boys, I'm separating you two." Carl wedged his chair in between Sam and Nate as if he were the responsible adult at the table.

Mila gave them a half-grin. "Sometimes I wish one of you would bring a girl over just so I wouldn't be bombarded with testosterone all the time."

"Well, if they did bring over some girls, you wouldn't be able to have me over for dinner anymore," Carl replied. "I mean, I'm so handsome, I would be stealing all their honeys all the time. I got mad rizz."

Mila let out a laugh as Sam backhanded Carl across his arm, shaking his head.

"Oh, yeah, remember when Carl stole Katie away from Nolan Brewster and then ghosted her the next day?" I asked.

Mila tilted her head and put her hands on her hips. "Carl?"

"Mrs. S, I only did it 'cause he said I couldn't." Carl pointed to Sam.

Mila shook her head with a smile, as she sat down next to her husband. "I think we better hurry up and say grace before the boys start acting up again."

Sam's dad nodded in agreement. His name was Yosef, but we called him Joe. He began to pray, thanking God for the food and His Son, which seemed odd because it didn't seem like that long ago that he had only prayed after dinner, and his prayer had never included the name Jesus.

After he said amen, he directed the conversation at Carl and me. "I have been wanting to talk to you boys about some things I've learned about the disappearances."

Our ears perked up, and for the first time in years, I felt a glimmer of hope in the pit of my stomach.

He kept on, "As you all may recall, a lot of other things were going on around the time your parents vanished. They may have seemed irrelevant at the time, but with a closer look, they are actually more related than you think." He started dragging on about politics in Europe, wars, the destruction of some city called Damascus, and the peace treaty in Israel that Gabriel Friedman, the secretary general of the United World Federation, had signed. "And tonight, there was an announcement that Gabriel Friedman will be making a trip to Jerusalem to visit the temple."

My glimmer of hope had changed to a more familiar feeling: the way I felt in history class when my teacher droned on about places I had never heard of or cared about. I wasn't even sure which continent Damascus was in, how hearing about it on the news a few years ago would have anything to do with my parents, or how Gabby Gabe—the nickname I used for Gabriel

Friedman because he liked to hear himself talk—could be related to all this.

Gabby Gabe was some political hero in Europe and had become more popular than the pope and president of the US combined. Besides him, I didn't know a single name of any leader of any country or organization besides our own president, but that didn't mean I cared about this guy's future plans to go to Jerusalem. It might have been a big deal, but I couldn't muster up enough energy to fake interest.

"You guys look bored, but I am saying all this because the Bible talks about a time when the church will be Raptured and—"

"You think my parents were Raptured?" I asked. "So you think I should just stop looking for them, that Carl should stop looking for his mom? What about that one couple who finally turned up in Colorado two years ago? Or the people who died and their bodies were found? If they were Raptured, how come they were found? Plus, it doesn't make sense. When I was a kid, I remember raising my hand in church when they asked if anyone wanted to be saved and not go to hell, so why wasn't I Raptured if that's where my parents went?"

The Rapture he was referring to was something I had heard about since I was little. It was the belief that Christ would come back for everyone who was a Christian. Essentially, they would vanish and be with God in Heaven. At least, that was how I'd understood it whenever my mom had brought it up.

Joe could tell I was upset, but he remained calm. "Raising your hand doesn't mean anything. Did you ever have a relationship with Jesus? Did you ever pray to Him or talk to Him? Did you ever ask Him for forgiveness? Your parents' disappearance is because they grew in grace with Christ by having that personal relationship that we missed out on."

The idea of talking to someone who didn't talk back to me or that I couldn't even see had always seemed odd. It wasn't that I didn't believe in God, it was just that I never gave it much thought.

"I need to warn you, boys, that as bad as things have been over the past couple of years, things are going to get worse, a lot worse. We are heading into what is called 'the great tribulation.' It is not going to be easy, but if you don't understand what has already happened, then it is going to be even harder. It's also very important to make sure you do not get the mark that Friedman has mandated. It is going to make things difficult for sure, but we have prepared ourselves here and are willing to help you boys out wherever we can."

I could see Carl holding back the tears. He'd only eaten half his plate, which was not like him at all. I knew he wanted to find his mom, but I also knew he had already come to this conclusion about the Rapture a while back. He hadn't been ready to fully accept it then, especially since no one else around him had. Sam, who had previously doubted the Rapture idea, now seemed to understand and believe what his dad was talking about. Max, however, clearly still held the belief that the disappearances had probably been the result of some mass alien abduction and didn't seem fazed by what Joe had said. There were dozens of different conspiracy-theory groups that all had their own crazy idea of what had happened, and Max bounced back and forth from one conspiracy to another depending on the mood he was in that day.

The lights started flickering, and the wind began to whistle outside.

"I think we better start heading back home," I changed the subject. "It looks like a big storm is coming, and I don't want to walk to the bus in this."

"Sam can take the car and take you home," Mila insisted.

People driving their own cars was getting less and less common, as the price of gas was around seventeen dollars a gallon on a good day, and there were huge oil shortages. Electric car batteries were becoming less popular and more a thing of the past because they did not last as long as they should have, and replacing them was way too expensive.

The Sterns had an older hybrid car. It was a 2023 silver-metallic Toyota Prius. The Sterns had bought it when they'd moved to the United States to give Nate a reliable car when he learned to drive. It was now a family car, and the Sterns had their own gas tank in the backyard from which they filled their cars and trucks for longer drives. I wasn't sure how much gas they had left, but they didn't drive much, so it seemed like one tank lasted months.

All vehicles had on-board units and were closely monitored through global navigation satellites, and everyone received a monthly toll bill in the mail based upon the number of miles they drove and what roads they used. Any money people saved on gas usually went to pay the tolls. Since bus transportation was free, that was what most people used. My parents both had cars that'd been left behind that I could drive, but frankly, I had never had much practice driving and hadn't thought about getting a license. Plus, neither of the cars were registered anymore.

I had planned to check whether or not the man in the Colts hat was still sitting in the same spot as we drove past the bus stop, but my mind was preoccupied with the words Joe had said over dinner. Did I have a "relationship" with God? How were things going to get worse, and to what extent? Had my parents been Raptured? The car ride back to my house was quiet, as if everyone else was pondering the same questions.

My mom had given me a Bible as a gift a couple of years before she'd disappeared. She'd said, "There may come a time when you start looking for answers. This will have the answers in more ways than one. Hopefully, you will start looking for them soon. I love you so much."

I hadn't given much thought to that gift since. I was fairly certain it was still in the box in my closet exactly where I'd put it the same day my mom had given it to me.

"Look, I know sometimes my dad sounds pretty straightforward, but I think you guys should give what he said some thought," Sam broke the silence. "He wouldn't say something if he didn't one hundred percent believe it himself. I've really learned a lot from him over the last few months."

"I know you all care about us like we're fam," Carl said. "It's just kind of cringe to think about. We're still here, ya know? That's rough."

Everyone became silent again, and the sound of the beating rain on the windshield put me into a trance. I didn't even notice Sam had already dropped off the other two when he pulled into my driveway. Sam gave me a half-grin as I slowly moved out of the car. I walked to my house in silence, ignoring the rain as it hit my face.

That night, I could barely sleep. I tossed and turned, thinking about all the things my mom had taught me about God and how I'd pretended to care while zoning out. Now, I wished I could remember what she had said. I missed her so much.

It was two in the morning before I finally started to drift off. I set my alarm for seven and started to lay back down, and the next thing I knew, my alarm was going off, reminding me why I hated getting up so early.

Chapter Three

I jumped out of bed on Thursday morning with the expectation that I was running late for school. I was throwing on my blue Grizzlies football shirt when I remembered that school was over and I was meeting Max this morning to ride with him to town and look around for some work.

My hand was on my wallet when I heard a knock on the door. Max stood on the porch with his Reds hat on, looking at his phone in one hand with his skateboard tucked under his other arm. I locked the door behind me, and we started walking toward the bus in silence. I guessed we'd both had very little sleep, as we were walking like a couple of zombies.

"How does it feel to finally be a grown up?" Max asked.

"Huh? Oh, you mean since I graduated? Heh, yeah, I guess I'm nervous about trying to get a job. Not sure how this will play out," I replied.

"I mean, you know I always have your back. If things get rough, we can always pool together and help each other out. What else are friends for, man?"

Max was right. I never had to worry about anything because my friends were always there for me.

The bus pulled up just as we arrived at the bus stop. I was happy to see Gary, as he always cheered me up.

Gary greeted me with his usual big smile. "Well, well, if it isn't Mr. Scott. I didn't expect to see you this morning. What are you doing up so early now that school is out?"

"Figured I would start the day off early to see if I can find some work," I replied.

"Sounds like a good plan. Don't forget this is the last day to use your old bus pass. Tomorrow, we will only be scanning your chips." Gary didn't sound excited to remind me of the inevitable, but he had a job to do.

Max and I sat down, and the ad with the joker-face lady started playing. Besides her annoying high-pitched voice, the ride was quiet, and I dozed off for a moment before the bus stopped. Max and I walked off the bus together about a block away from Neher's Body Shop where Max worked. We continued our slow pace, stepping heavily as if we were trodding through mud.

"I would kill for an energy drink right about now," Max broke the silence as we headed toward the shop, where Max had been working for about a year, ever since he'd graduated. "I haven't had one of those things in almost eight months."

"I could use one myself," I replied. "Tell you what, after I talk to your manager, I'll head down the street and grab us a couple of drinks. On me. Well, on my parents, that is." I figured I should use up whatever I had left in their account since I wouldn't be able to use my card starting tomorrow.

"Bet!" Max said, offering me a fist bump without raising his head from his phone.

Inside the office of the shop sat a girl, close to my age, with streaks of dark red through her dark brown hair, which was pulled up in a ponytail. She sat at a desk covered in papers and receipts. On the wall behind her was a "Don't Tread On Me" poster next to an *Atlas Shrugged* poster. She had on dark makeup and a nose piercing and wore plain shop clothes. "Can I help you?"

"Yeah, I hope. My name is Scott, and my buddy Max works here, and I was hoping you may have some extra work around here that I could do."

She chewed her gum while looking me up and down, appearing unimpressed. "You've ever worked on cars before?" she asked in a monotone voice.

"Uh, no," I replied.

"I see. You, uh, ever had a job before?"

"Um, er, not exactly."

"Okay. Well, do you have the mandatory chip so you can work?" She was beginning to sound exasperated by my very presence.

"Uh, no. I, uh, wasn't sure it was, umm, something I—"

"Look," she interrupted, "I get it. You want to find something to get you by so you can get stuff you need without having to get that chip or sounding off too many alarms. To be honest, I haven't gotten the chip yet myself. I literally got an advance on my check and sent all my creditors extra money to get me through the next couple months to give me some time to decide if I want the stupid thing or not. I decided I don't. I don't like people knowing my business, and I don't like the idea that I'm constantly being monitored, like I need parents all of a sudden when I haven't had any since I was fourteen, and I'm sure not going to pledge my undying love to that pompous leader."

"Did you lose your parents during the disappearances, too?" The words fell out of my mouth before I realized I had just implied, to a complete stranger, that my parents were missing.

She looked at me as if I was an idiot. "No, my parents divorced when I was fourteen, and neither of them seemed to want me in the divorce. I think the only thing they fought over was the liquor cabinet and all its contents, not like that is any of your business. But, yeah, I think I can help you out. Come back tomorrow at the same time, and I'll put you to work. It won't be much, and I will only be able to pay you with stuff that you could use to trade for now. Hopefully, you at least know how to use a broom."

"I can totally use a broom, and that's perfect! Thank you so much…uhh, I'm sorry, I didn't get your name."

"Audrey, Audrey Black. I'm the fill-in manager around here."

I gave her an awkward smile before saying, after a long pause, "Well, thanks, Audrey. I will see you tomorrow."

She lifted her eyebrows with a slight eye roll as if to say, *Yeah, right*. I was kind of drawn to her standoffishness. I bumped into the doorway on my way out of her office, turned with a smile, and put my hand up to indicate I was okay. "Uh, thanks again, Audrey."

She tried to hide the smile on her face with her hand.

I saw Max as I was heading out the front door of the shop and gave him a thumbs-up. He smiled and nodded, which was the first time I'd seen Max smile all week. I remembered my promise to get us energy drinks and headed toward the closest minimart, daydreaming about what tomorrow would look like at my new job. I thought about Audrey, too. She was beautiful enough to capture any man's attention but seemed reserved enough to keep them from approaching her. I was used to getting attention from girls at school, but their shallowness always deterred me from engaging them more than a friendly hello.

I was a block away from the store when I saw someone's shadow behind the next wall leading to an alleyway. People often stood outside their shops in the alleyway to smoke or take phone calls, so I didn't think anything of it until I saw a man with a Colts hat and dark sunglasses peek around the corner.

When he saw me, he turned back toward the alley. It sounded like he had taken off running. My instincts took over, and I ran after him. When I turned the corner, he was gone, but I could still hear his footsteps, so I continued down the alley. I thought I heard sounds coming from my right before the next turn, so I turned in that direction and immediately heard cans crashing behind me. I kept moving as I turned to look behind me. I thought I saw a man stumbling forward just as I smashed full force into someone standing in my path. We both tumbled to the ground.

I heard the person lying next to me let out a big *Humph* before saying, "What the heck? What are you running from, man? Are you okay?" It was Sam.

A man in a gray suit and red tie with what looked like a mustard stain on it stood over us and offered both of us a hand. It was Detective Clarke. Clarke had taken a lot of the disappearance cases, including Carl's mom's case. He was a tall, awkward man with graying blonde hair, and his breath smelled like coffee and cigars.

"Hey there, Scott, you alright, man?" Clarke asked. "What's the rush?"

"Sam, I am so sorry! I didn't see you guys. I thought I saw someone watching me, and when I went to confront him, he took off running."

Clarke's expression turned from amusement to concern. "Did he say anything to you? Did you get a good look at him?"

"Uh, no, I didn't, and no, he didn't try to approach me or anything. I know it sounds weird, but I've had this feeling like he's been following me for a while now, and I—"

Clarke interrupted me. "How long has he been following you?"

"I mean, I haven't actually seen him following me exactly, it's just that I see him around a lot, and it just feels like—"

"What does he look like, and where have you seen him?"

I almost felt like I was in trouble and Clarke was going to bring me down to the station for more questioning. "He is, like, six foot tall, and he always has on a Colts hat and sunglasses, so I've never actually seen his face. I've seen him around town and at the bus stop for the past couple of years, I guess."

"So let me get this straight," Clarke said. "You see some guy with a Colts hat, something worn by half the people in this city, hanging around town and at the bus stops, but he has never actually followed you home or to school or any specific place and has never approached you, and you just decided that today was the day you were going to chase him down? What were you going to do when you caught up with the guy?"

"I hadn't really given it much thought. I just thought that maybe I could get some answers." I felt pretty stupid. "Look, I am sorry, I really am. I wasn't thinking, and I didn't mean to run into Sam. I will catch up with you later, okay, Sam?"

Sam had been staring at me with a surprised look, clearly not sure what to say or think, but when I turned to go, he yelled out, "Achi, it's okay. I'm fine. You should come by for dinner tonight for sure."

I waved my hand behind me to confirm I would come. I rounded the corner to the minimart and went inside. My mind was still on the man in the Colts hat. I wandered around for a few minutes without realizing that the shelves were wiped out.

"Everyone is stocking up before tomorrow when the chip is mandated," the clerk said in a monotone voice, as if he was a computer that could read my mind. His chip was predominantly displayed in the middle of his forehead; people called it "The Mark" for this reason. He went about stocking the shelves as if I was not even in the store. I grabbed a few items and started to head out the store when the clerk said, "Thank you, may Friedman be with you." His saying caught me off guard, but I just smiled politely and left.

I headed back to Max's shop. He was busy but gave me another thumbs-up when I set his energy drink on the counter. Before I left, I caught a glimpse of Audrey. She was standing with a clipboard talking to another employee. I didn't realize I was staring until she looked up at me, raised her eyebrow, and gave me a curious crooked smile. I looked down quickly to end the awkward moment but turned back one more time before I left to see if she was still looking up at me. She was. I felt embarrassed, but she smiled bigger and put her hand up to wave bye. I smiled back and then finally left.

I headed to the Walmart to do some stocking up, planning to take several trips to the store and back to my house, as I wanted to make sure I had plenty of food, clothes, and other supplies before tomorrow. The bus ride would be a little dangerous with so many items, as people were often mugged for their groceries even with the surrounding facial recognition screens.

I usually did my shopping from home with my VR set. I would slip on the lenses, which made it look like I was in the grocery store. Any item I touched would go into a virtual basket. When I was finished, I would simply hit the end button, and my card would be charged and my selected items shipped to my house. I didn't usually know what I was looking for until I saw it, so I liked VR shopping better than regular online shopping.

I'd decided to go to the store in person this time so I could better look around. I felt like an adult making wise choices about the type of detergent and toothpaste I bought. I even managed to buy a four-thousand-watt gas-powered portable generator. I didn't have a clue what I would use it for, but I kept returning to the store, and the light at the exit kept turning green, indicating I hadn't run out of money, so I figured, why not? I was surprised because the prices were so high, and I'd spent so much money already. I'd thought the rest of my money would have run out pretty quickly. I knew families that had to work an entire day to be able to buy dinner that night.

When I was little, there had been people called *cashiers* that would take all the stuff you grabbed off the shelf and run it across a glass that would beep. My mom said when her grandparents had gone to the store, someone would have to enter by hand every item's price into a calculator. I couldn't imagine having to stand in a line just to get food. Now, people just walked into stores, took what they needed from the shelves, and walked right back out. If the light at the exit turned green, the door opened, and people's cards or chips were automatically charged. If the light turned red, the door didn't open, but I didn't know what happened after that since it had never happened to me before.

Most people didn't go into stores anymore, though, and instead did all their shopping online. There were also devices on refrigerators into which people could say what they needed, and those groceries would be delivered to their houses within the hour. Sometimes groceries were delivered by drones, but larger bulk items were delivered by driverless cars or trucks. I could have Pat order me items that I needed as well, but sometimes the orders got messed up, and I'd got random items. Once I'd been delivered twenty pounds of bananas instead of a single bunch.

I saw a young mother with a little boy walking around the store. They looked hungry but only had one loaf of bread in their basket as they headed out the exit. The lady didn't appear to have the chip either.

I quickly grabbed a few items from the food section and followed them out the door. "Excuse me, ma'am, I grabbed this stuff and decided I didn't need it. Would you guys be able to use this stuff?"

"Sorry, I don't have anything to pay you for it," the woman said, grabbing the little boy's hand.

"No, I don't need anything for it. I don't have the chip, and I was just trying to spend everything I have today." I held out the bag of food to her.

Tears welled up in her eyes. "I prayed that God would provide something for us today. I guess He answers prayers in ways you would never expect."

Her words made a lump form in my throat. I offered to get her more food, but she gratefully took the single bag and told me she needed to be somewhere.

After I had everything I could possibly need for the near future, I went back to the store a few more times to shop around for things that would be fun to have. I had never splurged on myself before in all these years alone, but this was probably my last chance to spend the money my parents had left, so I wanted to spend as much as I could.

I passed the sports section and decided to buy a bike, as I wasn't sure if I would be allowed on the bus after today. On my way up to the front door, I also grabbed a drone, which I'd always wanted to play with. As I walked back to the bus stop for what seemed like the hundredth time, I replayed the day's events in my head.

Why had Detective Clarke been there, and why had Sam been in that alley talking to him? Sam wasn't involved in any of the cases that Clarke took, at least none that I knew of, and there was no reason for Sam to have been in the area to have accidentally bumped into the detective. Detective Clarke had questioned me over three years ago when he'd questioned Carl, and he still remembered my name. He might just have had a great memory, but that seemed suspicious to me.

Later that evening, we all headed to Sam's house. I brought a couple bottles of detergent as a gift for Sam's parents for always making us dinner. Max thought it was odd, but I'd remembered Mila talking about how expensive detergent was getting, and when I handed her the bottles, she gave me a big hug and told me how thoughtful I was. I had about thirty more bottles at home and told her she could have more. I doubted I would ever use that much since I never had that much laundry.

Mila made us shakshuka from ingredients she had gathered from her greenhouse and eggs from the chickens. It was just spicy enough that my nose ran a little, but that didn't stop me from eating a second bowl and sopping up the juices with challah. Mila had braided the bread and coated it with butter before baking it; Joe often said the extra twenty pounds of weight he had put on was all challah.

We were all so busy stuffing our faces that it wasn't until Joe had finished his last bite that the silence was broken. "Thank you, my shefela, for this wonderful dinner tonight, as always!"

Mila smiled and blushed as she stood up from the table and started gathering plates. Sam had told me a long time ago that *shefela* meant sheep. I thought it was a weird thing for Joe to call Mila, but she seemed to think it was cute.

Carl was the first to jump up and help Mila. Living with his mom and then his aunt had made him more in the habit of helping as soon as dinner was over. I also started to get up but was stopped by Joe.

"You boys sit back down. Nate and Sam can help Mila for a bit." I looked at Sam, who was shoving Nate into the kitchen. "I'm sorry you both were upset last night. You must know that upsetting you isn't my intention, but I love you all as sons, and I want to make sure you not only know the truth but are prepared for what is to come as well." This time, his gaze was on Max. I was sure he could tell that Max was avoiding eye contact, but that didn't stop Joe's stare.

"I understand, Joe, sorry I got snippy with you last night," I replied. "I actually took a lot of what you said to heart and bought a bunch of supplies earlier today." Joe nodded but looked less than confident that I'd understood the severity of what he'd spoken of. "I remember my mom leaving me something, and I think I'm going to try to look for it when I get home tonight."

"Do you think I could come by and help you look for it?" Max asked.

Joe looked shocked at Max's interest. "That sounds like a great idea," Joe said.

"I'm totally in as well!" Carl said.

"Well, it looks like there is a search party at the Killian house tonight, I guess," I said with a snicker.

Before another word could be said, the sound of glass crashing came from all around the house. The cups on the dinner table were sloshing, and the chandelier was swaying, making the lights look like they were dancing around the room.

We all braced ourselves. The cracking of thunder sounded as soon as the earthquake was over. The rumbling continued in the distance as the rain came down hard and fast.

"It looks like I will be driving everyone over to your place again," Sam said.

"We should be very grateful for the weather. Lots of places overseas are having severe droughts right now," Joe reminded us.

"What did the cow say when it was swept up into the air by a tornado?" Carl asked.

We all just looked at him as if to say, *Don't do it.*

"I don't know, but it was an udder disaster!" Carl finished.

Moans were heard around the room, and even Joe winced and shook his head as if to say, *That was terrible.* Carl walked into the kitchen still laughing at his joke.

"Moooove it," Sam said to Carl, laughing as he shoved past him from the kitchen back to the dining room.

"You are all 'butchering' these jokes." I was proud of myself for continuing the cow pun, but Joe seemed to be the only one who understood the pun and cracked a smile.

"On that note, I think I'll go to my room," Nate said. He body-checked Sam then walked up the stairs.

Sam grabbed his car keys, and the rest of us said our goodbyes and headed to the garage.

Sam told everyone the story of when I'd chased the man in the Colts hat and ran into him. "He totally knocked the wind out of me, too! For what it's worth, though, I did see that man running, and Clarke and I thought it was totally weird, and I thought about seeing what was going on until I got pulverized. Scott, you should have played on the football team in high school."

We all chuckled.

"Detective Clarke was there?" Carl asked. "He called me a couple of weeks ago and asked me if I had heard of the Rapture theory. I thought it was odd because I hadn't heard from him in so long, but turns out he never stopped working on the case. He said he has been doing a lot of research on the Rapture theory and has come up with a lot of interesting information. He said he would keep in touch and to call him if I heard anything else. Then your dad mentioned it again last night."

"Interesting how some things all come to light sometimes," Sam said.

I was still curious as to why Sam had been meeting up with Clarke in the first place. Now that I had all these questions, it was time to start looking for some answers.

Chapter Four

The storm started coming in hard as Carl, Max, and I stepped out of the car. We could barely see the taillights as Sam drove off because of the torrential downpour. The ground was rumbling under our feet, whether from an earthquake or the thunder and lightning, we couldn't tell.

Just as we were entering the house, Sam pulled back up and parked diagonally in the driveway.

"I couldn't see a thing! I think I'll just chill out here for a while until this storm blows over!" Sam shouted. "I think my mom would rather me be safe here than for me to try and make curfew!"

We all laughed except for Max. He was quiet again, hiding his eyes with his Reds hat as if something was bothering him.

"Good evening, Scott, is there something I can assist you with?" Pat's screen turned on in the living room as we entered.

"Pat, turn on the lights, and turn off the air," I said as I reached for a towel with a shiver.

After we passed around the towel to dry off from what had seemed like a monsoon, we headed upstairs to my room. Carl threw himself down across my bed, Sam sat in my gaming chair, and Max stood in the corner against the wall with his arms crossed.

"Okay, so where do we start looking, and what exactly are we looking for?" Max asked.

"So I think it's in a small box that was put in a bigger box at the top of my closet, but I'm not completely sure." I grabbed my desk chair and stood on it in front of my closet, trying to reach the box I thought the Bible was in. Once I reached the box, I tossed a bunch of old trophies from the top of it to the ground then shuffled through the rest of its contents. No Bible. "Why don't one of you go over there and look for it on or in my desk?"

"Okay," Max replied, "but we still don't know *what* we are looking for."

"It's a small box with a Bible inside."

Max instantly stopped searching and looked as though he wanted to strangle me. "We are looking for a Bible? There are thousands of those things lying around everywhere in this town. You can probably go into any church and ask for one, and they will just give it to you for free."

"I know, but I think this one is different. My mom made it seem like this particular one would somehow help me more than any other would."

"Dude, I give up. There are Bibles literally everywhere. Not sure why we should be looking for one that you got years ago. Makes no sense." Max seemed agitated, as if I'd lured him here under false pretenses.

I reached for the second box on the shelf and sifted through a pile of clothes and stuff I never used anymore. I pulled out some old pictures of me with long hair and braces, and the guys all chuckled. When I reached back in, I felt something hard at the bottom of the box. "Here it is!"

The smaller box I pulled out still looked brand new. Inside it was the Bible, which I took out and opened for the first time. There was an envelope just inside the front cover. I felt immediate shame for never having opened something my mother had given me.

"There's an envelope with my name on it." I opened the envelope and took out the letter inside.

Everyone perked up, including Max. I was both excited and nervous to read the letter from my mom.

Scott, if you are reading this soon after I gave you this precious gift, I hope you find joy in reading God's word and learn to grow from it every day. If you are reading this and I have disappeared, please keep reading.

I looked up at everyone, and I was sure my face looked as shocked as theirs did. My skin felt flushed, and my heart was beating a thousand miles per hour. "Dude, you guys, I'm kind of freaking out right now." I kept reading.

I know this is a scary time for you. I often wondered if you and your father were saved. I would pray often for you both, but I know when I mentioned God to either of you, our conversations usually did not go anywhere. Your father started taking more of an interest lately, and I am still praying this is the change I had hoped for. If you are alone, I hope you will find someone who understands God's word and can explain to you what the Rapture is and why I am gone.

My stomach felt tied up in knots. My hands were sweaty and my mouth dry. Joe had been right. My eyes started to well up, but I didn't want to cry in front of my friends.

Before I could continue reading my mom's letter, a quiet creaking came from downstairs followed by a large *bang*. We all jumped, and my sadness turned into panic as shivers ran down the back of my neck. It was most definitely the back door. The closer on the screen door had broken a year ago, so if someone tried to sneak in, the door would slam behind them.

"Someone's in the house. No one has a key to this house except for me, and the back door is always locked. We have to get out of here now!"

"Someone is at the back door." Pat's voice came from the speaker downstairs.

"A little more of a heads-up, Pat," I mumbled in exasperation.

All four of us rushed to my bedroom window, which faced the front of the house. As Sam started to climb out the window onto the roof, I ran back to my open bedroom door. I could see a beam of light coming from a flashlight at the bottom of the stairs. I slammed the door shut, locked it, and threw my desk chair in front of it before returning to the window.

"Oh my goodness, oh my goodness, oh my goodness," Carl repeated to himself.

Sam was already jumping onto the ground from the roof. Carl was nervous about heights but was right behind him. When he slid himself down the side of the house from the roof, he landed on his ankle and twisted it. Before I could ask if he was okay, I heard the intruder running up the stairs. My heart had already been racing from my mom's letter, and now it seemed like it was going to pound right out of my chest. Max was on the roof when I heard the doorknob wiggle. I heard pounding as I started to climb through. I didn't look back. I couldn't.

Max and I both made our way down the ledge of the roof and onto the ground below. Running, we almost beat Carl, who was limping, to Sam's car. We all made it into the car, and as Sam backed up, I saw a figure looking down at us from my bedroom window. I couldn't make out his face, but he looked a lot like the man I had seen following me.

"Look! I think that's the man from the bus stop and the alley," I said.

Sam was so focused on getting out of the driveway he didn't have time to look. The car hurtled backward, and I almost hit my head on the dashboard when he threw the car into drive and slammed his foot on the gas.

Carl tried to look up but was sitting behind me. "I can't see anything but a silhouette."

"I didn't see him at all," Max said.

"I think that man has been following me and somehow knew I found the letter, like he's been eavesdropping on me somehow," I replied. "I mean, why would he start coming after me now?" I still had the Bible and the letter with me. "As soon as we get somewhere safe, I need to try to figure out why this is so important and read the rest of the letter."

"Maybe it isn't the letter. Maybe he came after you tonight because you chased him today. Just a thought," Max said.

Max may have been right, but the timing of everything had my head spinning. I should have been more careful. I had put my friends in jeopardy. I thought I was going to be sick.

"Pull over!" I cried. Sam pulled off to the side of the road. The rain from earlier had let up a little by the time we'd been climbing out the window and was now almost gone. I jumped out of the car and looked behind us. I didn't see anything. My hands hit my knees, and I bent over, trying to catch my breath. I thought I was going to pass out or throw up. "I just needed some fresh air real quick. I'm sorry, I would never have let you all come over if I thought that it would put you in danger."

"We are not blaming you at all, Scott. You are right, he does seem like he is after something extremely specific. He didn't start robbing the place downstairs. He came straight up to where we were standing," Sam said.

I had just regained my breath when I heard the screech of tires coming from around the corner. I stood up and saw headlights coming straight for us.

"Quick, get in!" Carl shouted. "GO, GO, GO!"

Sam hit the gas hard before I had even shut my door all the way.

"What do we do now?" Sam asked. "We can't just go to my house. He will follow us there, and I don't think he is the type of person you can reason with."

"I'm calling Detective Clarke," Carl said, pulling out his phone. He put the phone on speaker while it rang.

Sam was driving faster than I'd known he was capable, but the headlights were getting closer.

"Detective, it's me, Carl!"

"Hey, Carl, now's not a great—"

"We are in serious trouble! The guy that was following Scott chased us out of his house, and we are in a car, and he is getting closer—" The sudden crashing sound that came from the back of the car sounded worse than the cracking of thunder earlier. The man's car had hit the back of Sam's car, making us lose control. Sam's car turned sideways, and Carl let out a huge scream about two octaves higher than I'd ever heard his voice go.

"What was that? Carl? Carl, are you okay?" The phone had flown out of Carl's hands and onto the floor in front of him, but we could still hear Detective Clarke through it. "Hello? Guys, where are you?"

Sam managed to straighten the car and kept driving. The man behind us had to spin his car around, but he soon caught up again.

"He hit us! He hit us, and he is right behind us again!" Carl was frantic, and it was hard to understand what he was saying. His six-foot-five frame was so slouched down in the seat that I couldn't see his head through the rearview mirror. The phone was still by his feet.

"Okay, Carl, I need you to stay calm. Where are you, and can you head toward the station? I will meet you guys there."

"On it," yelled Sam as he jerked the steering wheel to the right, now heading in the wrong direction down a one-way street. The tires squealed, and we went off the road to the left. We hit a milk can, which spun in the air before hitting the side of the Salvage Sisters Antique Market.

The car behind us missed the turn, and as we continued the wrong way down Yandes Street, Max yelled, "I think we lost him!" while looking over his shoulder.

I could still hear its engine, so I turned to my left and spotted the other car. As we continued the chase, I could see the pursuing car at every intersection. Neither of us stopped at any of the stop signs, and at one point I thought we were going to hit a cat, but we barely missed it. Carl's deafening screams were constant. I knew if we kept going, the other car would cut us off on Cincinnati Street.

"Slow down and turn left at the next street!" I yelled.

"But that is heading right for him," Sam cried.

"Trust me!"

 Sam slowed down and made a sharp turn onto Ohio Street.

"Turn off your headlights!" I yelled.

Scott turned them off, and as soon as we hit the intersection, we all looked to our right. The other car was still barreling forward. Scott hit the gas, and we drove right past him without being noticed.

As we all gave big sighs of relief, Detective Clarke could be heard through Carl's phone. "Guys! Hello?"

"We are okay! We lost him. We will be there in five minutes."

Sam drove so fast we arrived at the station in less than four minutes. Detective Clarke was standing outside the station with a few patrol officers.

We sat in the car with our eyes wide, staring straight ahead as if we had all awoken from a bad dream. Clarke looked both worried and disappointed as he approached our car. I rolled my window down, and he bent over and looked in as if he were checking to confirm we were all in one piece.

"You guys mind telling me what that was all about?"

Chapter Five

The small office in the police station smelled like a mix of stale coffee, body odor, and shoe polish, and I was fairly certain that the four of us were putting out a third of that smell. We were all still breathing heavily, and sweat glistened over our faces.

Detective Clarke walked into the room. He looked like he'd only had a couple hours of sleep in the last two days. There were coffee stains splattered onto his shirt that accented the yellow mustard stain on his red tie.

We all started talking at once.

"Whoa! One at a time! I can't make out what anyone is saying." Detective Clarke looked like he was developing a migraine. "Carl, you go first. What happened tonight?"

Carl looked Detective Clarke directly in the eyes and made a big gulp in his throat. "We almost, I mean, I thought, I thought we were going to die." Carl paused. We all seemed to realize we were feeling the same way as Carl at that moment. "We had dinner at Sam's then went to Scott's house to look for something he remembered his mom left him." Carl continued to tell Detective Clarke what had happened that night. He even told him about the letter, which made me wince.

"So what did the letter from your mom say?" Detective Clarke looked extremely interested.

"We didn't get a chance to finish reading it, but she mentioned him reading it after she disappeared, like she knew it was going to happen." Carl blurted out the words before I had a chance to stop him.

"Wait, your mom disappeared?" Detective Clarke sounded like a parent ready to ground his child for the rest of their life. "Scott! Why didn't you report it? Is your dad missing, too?"

I nodded.

"Where is the letter now?" Detective Clarke demanded.

I pulled the letter from my pocket. I was reluctant to show anyone because I didn't know whom I could trust, but at this point, I didn't know what else to do. Detective Clarke reached for the letter, and I gave it to him.

As he read it, I had to fight back tears again. "'Scott, if you are reading this soon after I gave you this precious gift, I hope you find joy in reading God's word and learn to grow from it every day. If you are reading this and I have disappeared, please keep reading. I know this is a scary time for you. I often wondered if you and your father were saved. I would pray often for you both, but I know when I mentioned God to either of you, our conversations usually did not go anywhere. Your father started taking more of an interest lately, and I am still praying this is the change I had hoped for. If you are alone, I hope you will find someone who understands God's word and can explain to you what the Rapture is and why I am gone. More than anything, I hope that you can find God's love and build a relationship with Him through His Son Jesus. I also need to let you know that there are some other dangers you will face, and I will explain this, but I didn't know how safe it would be to include it in this letter, so I have hidden something for you in a place where I know you will find it. Ted will help you. I love you, Mom.'"

The five of us sat there, all reluctant to speak first. Detective Clarke looked both concerned and confused. "I can see why you may have thought the guy went after you for finding this letter. It seems pretty cryptic but may mean something pretty important. Although I am still not ruling out the possibility that he came after you because he figured you were onto him after the alley incident today. Scott, do you even know what any of this means?"

I shook my head, but I knew exactly what it meant.

"Scott, you need to think!" Detective Clarke seemed frustrated.

"I don't know," I shouted back.

Detective Clarke threw up his hands. "You boys need to get some sleep. Sam, we have already called your dad, and he should be here soon. Carl, we called and left a message with your aunt. If she doesn't call back, I can give you a ride home myself. Max, you need to get ahold of someone to pick you up. I didn't have any contacts for you. Scott, we will have a patrol car take you home and another car stationed outside your house."

I did not like the idea that I would be going home alone in a patrol car while another watched me. How was I supposed to know that the officers weren't working with the man in the Colts hat? But I was anxious to go back home and look for the rest of what my mom had left me.

Max was the first person to get up. He came to where I was sitting. "You know, no one is blaming you for what happened tonight. You okay, though?"

I didn't know how to answer that. I was physically fine, but my emotions were a mess, my mind whirling with a million what-if scenarios. All I could mutter was, "Yeah, man, I'm cool." I didn't want my friends to be worried. I wanted to be strong for them just like they'd always been strong for me.

One by one, we left the office. Max was the first to be picked up, and soon after Joe pulled up to pick up Sam. "I'm glad you boys are okay. It would not be a problem if you wanted to come stay with us for a while."

I was glad he'd offered, but I still had a million questions I needed to find the answers to. "Thank you, I'm sure there will be times that I take you up on your offer, but I need to get back home." I didn't want to say more than that because I didn't want anyone to be suspicious that I knew what my mom's letter had meant.

After my friends had all been picked up, an officer took me home. When he pulled up to my house, I saw the window to my room was still open, and it made my heart race just looking at it.

"We will do a quick perimeter search, and then we will be out front in our patrol car the rest of the night. If you need anything, just let us know." The officer seemed nice, but I had never met him before, so I simply nodded and went inside.

"Good evening, Scott. Is there anything I can assist you with?" Pat's humanlike voice made me jump. That was the first time it had ever startled me.

As the officers looked around outside, I walked toward the back of the kitchen. It didn't look like there'd been a break-in. The door to the kitchen was closed and unlocked but didn't look tampered with. I grabbed a heavy white shelving unit from the laundry room and blocked the door with it before heading back upstairs.

On the floor of my bedroom was the box from my closet with stuff strewn around it. My old teddy bear had been cut open and had the stuffing ripped out. Someone had come back to search for what had been written about in the letter. There was only one problem. They'd had the wrong Ted. I couldn't wrap my head around who could have come up here while we'd been sitting in the station. My paranoia was quickly turning into reasonable suspicion, but I didn't know who to be suspicious of.

I grabbed the letter from my pocket. *I have hidden something for you in a place where I know you will find it. Ted will help you.* I looked through my stuff on the floor. My mom had given me the now ripped-up teddy bear when I was five. At the time, I hadn't liked carrying it around because the other kids would make fun of me, but I'd loved my mom and hadn't wanted to hurt her feelings. My mom had heard the boys one day and come up to my room. She'd handed me a small model car, the doors and trunk of which opened. *Here, I named him Ted after your teddy bear. This way, you can carry him around with you instead and leave your bear here to be safe on your bed. You can also hide things inside like messages. Look!* I'd opened the trunk and found a little piece of paper that said *I love you* on it. My mom and I would write notes back and forth and hide them inside Ted's trunk all the time. Sometimes they would just say *Hi!*, but that one word had been enough for me to know she was there and always thinking of me.

I reached under my mattress for the first time in years and pulled out the yellow diecast Oldsmobile, Ted. I opened the trunk of the car, and inside was a key. My eyes filled up with tears, and this time I had no reason to hold them back. My mom had always put me before herself. Even when she'd known she would be gone and wouldn't have to worry about any of the troubles in this world, she had still wanted to make sure I was okay.

I knew the safe box this key went to was hidden outside in the floorboards of the shed. I would have to wait until tomorrow so the patrol officer wouldn't notice anything suspicious. For now, I needed to try to get some sleep. I didn't expect to fall asleep quickly, as my mind was spinning from everything that had happened, but I was physically exhausted, and the moment I laid in bed, I dozed off without setting an alarm.

Light shone through my window early Friday morning, hitting my face, which was half buried in my pillow. My drool had soaked my pillowcase, wetting the right side of my face. For a moment, I felt lost in time, not knowing what day it was, then panic set in. I was supposed to be at the shop this morning with Max!

I still had on the same clothes as the day before, but I didn't have time to change. I grabbed the bottle of mouthwash and swished some around my mouth as I ran down the stairs. As soon as I stepped foot outside, I spit the mouthwash onto the ground. When I looked back up, I noticed the patrol officer staring at me. I thought about telling him where I was going but figured it would just slow me down. It was already 7:45, and I'd been in Audrey's office yesterday at 7:30. I wondered if she'd even notice I was late.

I ran down the street toward the bus stop. Max was nowhere around. I wondered if he'd come by the house this morning and I hadn't heard him knocking, or maybe he'd kept walking when he'd seen the patrol officer. Most of the monitors around the bus station were playing tributes to Gabby Gabe instead of advertisements because he'd finally taken care of the two witnesses: "The whole world is celebrating as they look into the streets of the dead bodies of the doomsday duo."

The bus pulled up, and Gary opened the door.

"Hey, Gary."

"Hello, Mr. Scott, did you end up getting the mark yesterday?"

I had totally forgotten about the chip. "Oof. I woke up late, and I left the house in such a hurry, I totally forgot what day it was or that I couldn't use my bus pass today."

"Yeah, I didn't want to tell you how rough you looked," Gary said with a chuckle. "Come on in and stand up front. I don't think the facial recognition screens will be able to see you if you stand right there."

"Thanks, Gary. I was supposed to start my new job today, and I'm already late."

"I sure do wish you luck, Mr. Scott. It looks like you may need it," Gary said, pointing to my shirt, which prominently displayed mouthwash spit.

For the entire bus ride, I stood as close to the front of the bus as I could so I wouldn't trigger any ads. When I got off at my stop, I called behind me, "Thanks again, Gary. I'll see you in a few hours!"

"See you later, kid, I look forward to hearing all about your first day."

I ran down the street toward the shop. Max was already inside working. He didn't notice me walking in.

"Well, look who decided to show up." Audrey was standing in her office when I walked in. Her dark hair was down and fell around her face. The shop clothes she'd worn the day before had been replaced with a *V for Vendetta* t-shirt, jeans, and jungle-green windbreaker.

"I am so sorry. I had a, well, let's just say an interesting night last night."

"Yeah, your friend Max filled me in a little. To be honest, I didn't even think you would show up today." Audrey seemed genuinely sympathetic, which made me feel worse about being late. "To be honest, I was hoping you wouldn't come."

Her words cut me like a knife. I wasn't sure why I was so hurt by someone I had only met once for about five minutes.

"Look, it's not that I am not happy you are here or anything," Audrey continued, "it's just that my boss came in here after you left yesterday and told me that we wouldn't be able to hire anyone without the chip after all. I felt bad for telling you to come in today and realized I never got any phone number for you. I tried to call Max, but he didn't answer, and when you didn't come in with him this morning, I thought you weren't coming. To be honest, it looks like it's going to be my last day here. He told me I had till the end of the day to figure my stuff out and decide if I am going to get the chip. I was actually in the middle of packing up when you walked in."

"I'm so sorry to hear that. Do you have any idea what you will do?" I asked. She seemed to be at home here, and it didn't sound like she was very close to her parents.

"I should be okay for a bit. I met some people who are kind of in the same boat as I am, so we have a thing going. You know, I could introduce you to them, and maybe you can, like, I don't know, join our little circle or something. We meet up at least once a week." Audrey sounded nervous all of a sudden.

"I am super flattered that you thought of me and helped me out like that and all, and I would love to do that sometime, but right now I have a problem I need to solve." I didn't want to turn down her offer, but I didn't want to join into a group of people I didn't know when I wasn't even sure whom I could trust in the group of people I did know.

She looked sad as she threw what appeared to be her last remaining item from the office into her box. "Just be careful, okay?" She picked up her box and headed to the door.

"Which way are you heading?" I asked, following her out of the office. "Maybe I can walk with you for a while."

She gave me a half-smile and pointed in the direction of the bus station. "My street is about a block past the station."

"Sweet, I'm walking back that way."

We walked in silence most of the way to the station. My hands were sweating, and I felt my heartbeat picking up as I tried to think of something to talk about.

"I have a hard time trusting people, too," she said, as though she had read my mind.

"Am I that transparent?" I asked her with a chuckle.

"I can read you like a book." For the first time, I saw her laugh, and it made me feel warm inside.

The bus was pulling into the station just as we approached it, but when I walked up to the door and it opened, it was not Gary driving. "Uh, hi, where's Gary?"

"Gary doesn't work here anymore." The driver was very matter of fact and didn't crack a hint of a smile.

"Oh! I just saw him this morning, and he said he would see me later. Do you know where he went?"

He squinted at me as if studying my face. "What's your name, son?" He grabbed his CB radio and asked for assistance, but I started walking away as fast as I could, so I didn't hear what he said next.

"What was that all about?" Audrey looked more confused than scared, walking quickly to match my pace.

I followed her to her house, too panicked to reply, and we went inside. It was a small, older house with large trees in the front and a worn-down fence around the yard. The grass was well taken care of, and the inside was bare but clean. It looked like Audrey could have just moved in yesterday.

"I rode the bus this morning," I gasped, finally able to speak now that we were safely inside.

"So you ride the bus every morning?" Audrey replied.

"Yes, but this morning, the driver, Gary, let me ride even though I didn't have the chip. He let me stand in front of the bus, and now he is gone. He told me he would see me later, which means I don't think he was planning on quitting or leaving any time soon."

"You think they fired him for letting you ride the bus for free when it is free anyway?" Audrey asked, somewhat sarcastically.

"Actually, that is exactly what I think happened. For as long as I have known Gary, he has never missed a day of work, and he seemed fine this morning. He had me stand at the front of the bus intentionally so that I would not be scanned. What if he was fired because of me? Plus, this whole chip thing seems to be getting out of hand real fast."

Chapter Six

Audrey and I sat down on her couch discussing what we thought had happened to Gary. The couch was soft and pillowy, and I started to realize how tired I was. We sat for just a few minutes before we heard a knock on the front door. Audrey looked like she had seen a ghost.

"By the look of your face, I take it you aren't expecting any company?"

"No one ever comes here. None of my friends even know where I live. You are the first person to come over here. I don't spend a whole lot of my time here, and no one ever knocks on the door." Audrey sounded breathy and panicky.

I stood up to look out the window. "It's Detective Clarke! What is he doing here?"

"A detective? Scott, I think we should leave," Audrey whispered.

I agreed with her. I wasn't sure I could trust Detective Clarke after someone had come to my house last night and cut open my teddy bear just after Detective Clarke had read the name *Ted* in my mom's letter. "I suppose the bus driver may have radioed the police since I was on the bus when I shouldn't have been, but I'm not sure why that is a police matter."

The knocking on the door persisted. "Scott, I know you're in there. Open up! We need to talk."

"Do you have a back door?" I asked.

"Yeah, follow me." Audrey took off toward the back of the house, and I followed close behind, hearing Detective Clarke yelling my name at the front door.

Audrey and I looked around before opening the door and running toward the fence. The dew was still on the grass, and our feet got wet as we ran. We hopped over the fence into the neighbor's yard and didn't stop running until we thought we were far enough away that we couldn't have been followed. The patrol car would still be outside my house watching it, so I wasn't sure that was the best place for us to go next. I knew I had to get back to use the key my mom had left me, but I didn't want to put anyone else in jeopardy.

"Where are we heading?" Audrey sounded scared. Her hard shell and tough demeanor had melted away before my eyes.

"My friend Carl's house. I know I can trust him, and I need another pair of ears to bounce ideas off—" As soon the words fell out of my mouth, a realization hit me.

"What is it?" Audrey asked.

"Another pair of ears! What if none of my friends betrayed me, what if someone has been listening to me through my phone or something?"

"What do you mean 'betrayed you'?"

I still didn't know whom I could trust, but I wanted to trust her. "Well, my parents have been missing since a bunch of people disappeared a few years ago. I found a letter from my mom that has something to do with the disappearances, but people have been chasing me and following me ever since I found the letter, and they seem to know what the letter said somehow."

"Why didn't you tell me people had been chasing you before I brought you over to my house?" Audrey sounded mad.

I hadn't considered that I was putting her in harm's way when I'd walked with her. I felt terrible.

"I am so sorry. I didn't think we would be in danger, and while we were walking and talking, I was feeling so content and happy I forgot people were even following me until we arrived at the bus." I felt embarrassed that I'd shared that I was happy talking to her, but she immediately blushed and didn't seem angry at me anymore.

We continued walking to Carl's house, avoiding bus stops and facial recognition screens. When we passed by my house, we cut through my neighbors' backyards. The grass was overgrown through several of the yards, and we were able to move through them unnoticed. The patrol car was still sitting outside my house and was now accompanied by another police vehicle.

I pointed to a large coniferous tree that stood by the fence across the street from my house. "Stay over there for a second. I have an idea."

"Scott, no!" Audrey whispered, but I was already crouched down and heading toward the patrol cars. The officers from one car were outside of it doing a perimeter search, and the officers in the other car were looking at their phones. I quickly emptied my pockets into the cowl of the empty police car and ran back to Audrey.

"What was that all about?" Audrey asked.

"If it works, I'll tell you later," I said, giving her a half-smile and a wink. She blushed again, and I may have blushed back that time.

I crouched back down to cross the neighbor's backyard, Audrey close behind me. One of the neighborhood dogs was in the backyard and started to bark, so I picked him up to keep him quiet and kept on walking with him in my arms. Luckily, he was a small Boston terrier. I carried him the rest of the way to Carl's house. He seemed more than happy to be brought along.

I knocked on the back door of Carl's house, and as soon as Carl opened the door, I put my finger to my lips with my left hand to tell him it wasn't safe to talk. I was still cradling the dog with my right hand. Carl looked confused but went along. Inside, I set my phone on the dining table and motioned for Audrey and Carl to do the same, then I pointed upstairs.

Carl was the last to walk into his room, and as soon as he shut the door, he whispered, "Scott, what is going on? I've been trying to get ahold of you all day. And why do you have a dog?"

"Who? This? This is Boots. He is one of the dogs that hangs out in the neighborhood." I held Boots up to Carl's face.

Carl shook his head and turned his attention to Audrey. "Okay, then, who the heck is this? One of the stray girls that runs around the neighborhood?"

Audrey didn't seem amused but introduced herself anyway. "I'm Audrey Black, I'm Scott's, uh, um, friend. I mean, we just met, well, kind of. He was going to work for me, but I got fired, and, well, we ended up running from someone together. Actually, I don't really know what's going on either."

Carl threw up his hands and stared at me.

"Okay, look, I'm sorry, but this has been a crazy day," I said. "Someone was in my house last night. They had been searching for the missing piece that my mom mentioned in the letter. Oh, and I found a key."

Carl and Audrey looked at each other and then back at me in surprise. "A key to what?" Carl asked loudly.

"Shhhh, it's a key to a safe my mom and I used to use for top-secret stuff when we played spy games together when I was, like, nine. She hid the key in my toy car named Ted. The letter said Ted would help me. I know where the safe is, but there are patrol cars around the house, and I think the police are after me now. Detective Clarke showed up at Audrey's house pounding on her door just minutes after we arrived at her house."

"You were at her house?" Carl sounded both mad and shocked but then shook his head again and changed the subject. "Look, Detective Clarke was fired this morning. That was why I was trying to get ahold of you. My aunt called down to the station to thank him for helping us last night, but they told her he was no longer employed with the police department."

"Maybe I should have talked to him. He yelled my name when he knocked on the door and said we needed to talk." My mind was going a hundred miles a minute trying to piece the puzzle together. "Either way, we need to get to my house and get to that safe. Carl, you can head over there and knock on the front door. Pretend that you assume I am home and you're coming to check on me. That may distract them enough to keep their eyes off me when I go around back. I will leave my phone here. They may be tracking me even though I have my location turned off. Audrey—"

I paused. I hadn't even asked if she was willing to go along with our plan, but I needed her help, and I hoped she wanted to give it.

"Audrey," I continued, "is there any way you could take Carl's bike to this address?" I wrote Sam's address on a piece of paper. "There is a family who lives here that I can trust. Tell them that I need them to send Sam in the car to pick up me and Carl and to park across the street from Max's house. He will know where to go. After I open the safe, we will head in that direction and hide behind the abandoned house that is next to Max's. Can you do that?"

Audrey stared into my eyes and nodded. She looked concerned but also happy to be a part of something. We headed down the stairs and remained quiet. Audrey waved goodbye as she took Carl's bike then headed down the street.

Carl turned toward me. "Are you ready, man?"

I lifted Boots up to his face again. "Yes, we are!" Boots gave a little grunt. "That's right, Boots!" I said as Carl's disapproving look held onto my face.

We both headed toward my house. "Okay, Carl, this is where we separate. I will walk behind the houses, and you take the street. Walk at the same pace that we were just walking. We should hit the house at the same time."

"I gotchu," Carl said, holding up his fist to offer me a fist bump. "But after this is all over, you gonna tell me *all* about your new girlfriend!"

I wanted to protest that she wasn't my girlfriend, but all I could do was blush and shake my head. "Get out of here, punk." I withdrew my fist bump and punched Carl on the arm instead.

"See you on the other side," Carl snickered as he walked away.

Boots and I walked through a series of backyards on the way to my house and came across Inspector Bucket in his usual napping spot. "Come on, boy." I let out a whistle, and Inspector Bucket jumped up and followed me and Boots. Every now and then, we caught a glimpse of Carl through the fences or trees walking down the sidewalk toward the house.

When I was close enough to see the shed in my backyard, I felt a rush of adrenaline course through my body. I didn't see any officers in the back, and I could hear Carl knocking on the front door. I ran toward the shed and inside. The shed was large enough to have a workspace for projects. It was in good shape, but I hadn't used it much in the last few years. The floorboards looked untampered with as I knelt down to shimmy one of them loose. There was the safe. I reached into my pocket for the key, but as I pulled it out, it slipped from my fingers and fell between the safe and the ground. I could hear the officers talking to Carl, but I couldn't quite make out what they were saying. I reached down and could touch the key but couldn't grasp it between my fingers. "Come on!" I could hear a couple of the officers getting closer; they were coming around the side of the house.

"Let's do a perimeter check of the shed and around the back."

I turned to Inspector Bucket. "Go find your treat!"

Bucket had a great nose, and we would often play games where I would hide his treats and he would go search for them. The moment I said *treat*, Bucket took off running with Boots following close behind him.

"Where did these dogs come from? Hey, get down from there!" I could hear the officers' voices trailing off as they headed back toward their car where Bucket had run. Bucket jumped up on the hood and started eating the treats I'd hidden for him when I'd emptied my pockets earlier.

I managed to grab the key and opened the safe. Inside it was an envelope. I grabbed it and put the floorboards back as quickly as possible. I could hear the officers' voices getting louder again as they started walking back around the side of the house.

"Hey!" It was Carl. "I just wanted to let you guys know that you are doing an amazing job, and we all appreciate everything you do."

I poked my head out of the shed and saw both officers' backs were toward me as they looked at Carl.

"Uh, thanks, kid, but you should get back home," one of the officers said as I tried to make a run for it.

He started to turn back around, and I heard Carl shout, "But my aunt really wanted me to make sure to say thank you! Plus, I have always wanted to be a cop just like you!"

"Ah, thanks buddy." The cop sounded flattered. "If you like, I could show you our scanner." The officer was showing Carl something while I crossed the tree line. I made eye contact with Carl and nodded as I ran.

"Uh, thanks, but I gotta go. My aunt will be looking for me soon. Bye." Carl headed back toward the street, leaving the officer shaking his head.

"Dumb kids. He doesn't even have the mark yet, and he thinks he is going to be a cop."

As I ran in the direction of Max's house, I again could see Carl through the tree line on the street, but when I tried to signal to him, I heard a noise coming from behind me. I turned and saw the man in the Colts hat running after me. I picked up the pace, running toward Carl while jumping over hedges and dodging trash cans. I hit the sidewalk, grabbed Carl's arm, and pulled him back behind the houses. Carl looked over his shoulder to see why I was panicked.

"Not again!" Carl yelled.

This time, we were on foot, and Carl and I were much faster than the stranger chasing us.

"Oh God, please have Sam waiting for us when we get to Max's!" I had never prayed before, but I was starting to get the urge to talk to God, to tell Him how I felt, to release the guilt and emotional baggage I had been storing up inside me for so long. For now, I only had time to ask for help.

We cut through the yards of a couple of houses a block away from Max's house while heading back toward the street, and the man did the same behind us.

I saw Sam's car sitting on the side of the road. "Thank you!"

Carl looked at me with a smile that said, *I'm going to kick your butt!* and started running faster than I'd known he could. I started running faster, too. I could hear the man trailing farther behind us. My feet hit the pavement so hard my knees started to ache. I turned to look behind us and saw that the man had stopped running and stood in the street catching his breath. I also saw Inspector Bucket running behind him in our direction and then quickly passing him.

"Yalla!" Sam yelled as Carl and I jumped into the back seat of Sam's car.

"LET'S GO!" Before I could shut the door, Inspector Bucket jumped into the car. "Good boy, Bucket!"

Audrey turned around and faced me from the front seat and smiled. I smiled back and nodded in thanks.

"Where to, boss?" Sam asked.

I reached into my pocket, opened the letter, and said, "Seymour, Indiana."

<u>Chapter Seven</u>

Seymour, Indiana, was a town just a little smaller than Franklin and a little less than an hour south of where we were. I was anxious to get there, but I was also enjoying the downtime that riding in the car afforded us. We took US 31 south to avoid the interstate, where there were more patrol cars, and we jumped between side streets and back roads to make sure no one was following us. The trip, therefore, was taking longer than an hour, and I was getting pretty hungry.

"Here, I grabbed some snacks from Sam's house before we headed back to Max's to get you. I know it isn't much, but it was all I could grab in a hurry," Audrey said as if she'd read my mind, handing us Sam's lunch box, which was a blue box that looked like a Tardis. It was filled with peanut butter sandwiches, bags of chips, and packaged cupcakes.

"Woah, there's a lot of food in here," I said.

"It's bigger on the inside," Sam snorted, raising his head to look at Carl in the rearview mirror.

Carl looked back at Sam and shook his head in response.

"Sam's mom had some sandwiches already made up and told me to take them and she could make more," Audrey replied, ignoring Sam's joke, which he seemed to be enjoying more than the rest of us.

"Ah, thanks!" I exclaimed. "You're awesome!"

Carl snapped his neck around to look at me and raised his eyebrows up and down. I threw a package of cupcakes at his head, and he pursed his lips to make a kissy face at me. Bucket sat in between Carl and I and seemed to want the cupcake I'd thrown, so I gave him half of my peanut butter sandwich, and it was gone in one bite. He licked my face as if to say, *Thank you,* then rested his head on my lap.

"I didn't know you and Sam were friends," Audrey said.

"Wait, you know Sam?" I was shocked that Sam had any friends I didn't know about.

"Yeah, we go to the same Bible study," Audrey replied.

Sam and his parents had invited all of us every week to go to their Bible study, and I had gone once. It had just been Sam's family, myself, and Carl, making it seem like a family devotion time, so I'd felt awkward and never gone again.

"You go to Bible study?"

Audrey looked slightly offended by my question. "I was going through some depression." She sighed. "I started leaning on alcohol the same way my parents did all my life. I knew that I didn't want to turn out the way they did, so I made a conscious decision to end my life. The next thing I knew, there was a boy that had run out into the middle of the street chasing after a paper airplane. I ran after him and pulled him out of the way of a truck that was barreling toward him. I knew at that moment that God didn't send me to save the boy, but rather God sent the boy to save me. I was repentant and knew that I needed forgiveness more than anything. I started looking for answers and ran into Sam the next day at the minimart near the shop, and he invited me to their Bible study. That is the group of people I mentioned when we were on the way to the bus stop earlier that I wanted to introduce you to, but since you said you had some problems to solve first, I thought I would just ask you again later."

I could see Sam looking at me from the rearview mirror. It seemed like God put people in our path to help us along the way, and I was grateful for each and every one of the people He had put into my path, past and present. I felt guilty for always blowing people off when they were reaching out to help me. I had done it to my parents, and now I realized I had been doing it to my friends.

I guessed Sam could see I was struggling to say anything, as he changed the subject. "Hey, I need to let my parents know we are safe and what is going on, but Audrey told me we need to be discreet in what we say over the phone or through text. Oh, and we all turned off our locations. My mom knows we are going to be cryptic."

"Yeah, I think for now, I would rather be safe than sorry. I'm still trying to figure out who is following us and how they are getting their information. The guy in the Colts hat seemed to be waiting close to the house for me to come back but also seemed to be out of sight from the patrol cars, so I don't think they were working together since he followed us alone," I replied.

"So what was in the safe?" Carl asked.

"It was just an envelope holding a key and a note with an address and a map. Here." I passed the note to Sam. "I left my phone at Carl's house, and to be honest, I feel better without it."

As if on cue, Carl's phone began to ring. "It's Max. Hello…. Yeah, sorry, man, we kind of had a run in. We left town, but that is all I can say for now…. Well, Scott seems to think that people can listen to our conversations on the phone since people keep showing up in the worst places for us…. I know we can trust you, but we can't talk over the phone. Hold on, let me put you on speaker phone so the rest of them can hear you."

"I just want to know where you all went," Max said, sounding like he felt left out. "I saw you come into the shop, and then when I went to the office, you and Audrey were both gone. I went back to work thinking she was showing you around, but then after a couple hours I started to worry."

"Sorry, man, it's a long story, but we are all good." I didn't want to say too much, but I didn't want him to worry, either.

"Bro, where are you at?" Max asked.

"Can't say right now, but we are safe," I replied.

"Do you have your phone? I tried calling you, like, ten times, but I never got an answer." Max sounded annoyed.

"No, I left it at Carl's house. I don't think I will be using it any time soon. I think it causes more problems than it helps, to be honest."

"I'll meet up with you guys. Just tell me where to meet you. Is Audrey with you?" Max asked.

"Look, as soon as I figure out where a safe place to meet up is and a way to tell you, I will get back to you. I promise. For now, you are just going to have to trust me that we are safe and we will meet up with you soon. I just want to make sure you are safe, too, and the less you know right now, the better off you are." I didn't answer his question about Audrey because she looked at me and shook her head. I knew she also liked her privacy and had trust issues. "Sorry again, man, I'll talk to you later."

With that, Carl ended the call.

I took Sam's phone and texted Mila. *Hey, Mom, just watching a movie. You know that old set of movies we were watching with Scott, well, we decided to seemore today. Be back late. Love you.* Mila was smart, so I thought she could figure out that we were all together heading to Seymour and would be back later. If not, at least she would know Sam was okay.

"Hey, guys, I think we're here," Sam said, pulling into the parking lot of a storage unit facility.

I looked down at the key. On it was the number 3876. "Keep going all the way to the end," I said, careful not to say the number out loud. "There!" I pointed to the unit marked 3850-3910.

We parked the car and walked toward the cinderblock building. Inspector Bucket came with us, sticking by my side with every step.

"Looks like you have a new best friend," Carl said.

"I think I may have to keep him now. I mean, he and Boots kind of saved our butts back there. I owe him," I replied. "Plus, I think I enjoy his company more than he enjoys mine."

The units were old, and a rotten smell permeated the air, coming from inside units that'd been abandoned for years. Owners used to auction off their units, but since the disappearances and the increased death rate around the world, houses and items were more commonly abandoned and either left untouched or ransacked. Some towns and cities thrived as people left their decimated towns to move to ones that were flourishing.

Most of Seymour was abandoned. Previous Seymour residents that hadn't been affected by the disappearances had moved to more populated areas. There was a tall, faded mural on one of the buildings in town of the singer John Mellencamp, a favorite of my grandpa's, below which was the caption, *I was born in a small town*. The chipped paint and cracked bricks were anything but reminiscent of this town that had once taken immense pride in its people.

Weeds sprouted up through the gravel below our feet, and trash blew across the lot to find a permanent home against the weathered fence. When we reached the building, we walked in and down a long dark hallway of storage units. The air was damp, and the overhead lights made a *tink tink tink* sound as they flickered.

"This looks like the beginning of one of those scary movies where all the characters get picked off one by one," Carl whimpered.

I started to laugh, but when I looked at Carl, whose eyes were wide with apprehension, I realized he was only partly joking.

The first twenty units were in the first hallway, and the next ten were in the back hallway. Bucket walked ahead of us as if he knew where to go and was trailblazing the way for our safety. We rounded the corner, and the lights went out for a few seconds. On either side of me, Carl and Audrey each clutched one of my arms. When the lights flickered back on, Sam, who was behind us, let out a huge guffaw. Carl jumped back and pushed my arm away as if I'd made him grab it, and Audrey shyly looked at me with an awkward grin, blushing, as she let go of my arm.

"Okay, here it is." I opened unit 3876 with the key. The door made a loud grinding noise as it opened. My heart beat fast as I anticipated what we would find inside.

In the back, there were boxes of supplies and food storage. Against the left-side wall was a desk beside some filing cabinets, and against the right-side wall was a cot. It was obvious that no one had been here in several years.

I walked over to the desk. On top of it was a scatter of files and papers with *Killian Tech Innovations*, my dad's company, typed across the top. We all started going through sections of the unit. Sam sat at the desk while Carl and Bucket looked through the food. Audrey and I looked through some of the supply boxes.

Only about fifteen minutes had passed when we heard a loud "WHOA!" Sam's dark eyes were wide in disbelief. He sounded not only surprised but concerned as well. He was holding one of the documents from the desk.

"What is it? Did you find something?" Carl asked as he scooped a spoonful of peanut butter out of the tub he had found and started eating it. Audrey and I winced. "What? I wath hungry!" His *s*'s stuck to the roof of his mouth. Carl stuck his finger back into the peanut butter and gave some to Bucket, who gladly accepted the offer.

"Uh, yeah, you could say that I found something," Sam replied. "Did your dad go to Dubai several years ago?"

"I remember him talking about traveling to some convention or something when I was younger, but I can't for sure remember if it was Dubai. He seemed to travel a lot for work. Now that I'm thinking about it, he may have gone there a few times. Why?"

"Well, it looks like he was there representing his company to work with some of the other leading tech companies on quantum technology at the World Expo. At first, I thought this stuff was fascinating, but then I saw some more alarming stuff they were starting in Dubai," Sam replied.

"Like what?" I asked.

"Like this here is talking about the chips that are inserted into people's hands and foreheads, but it goes into a lot more detail than what they are offering on the news. The one inserted into the forehead actually elicits activity in a neural network. In fact, it causes synaptic alterations and behavior modifications by altering parts in the neural circuitry. This cannot be good. There is a way for them to cause a disruption of very specific molecular mechanisms, and here it shows an elimination of neurons," Sam said, pointing at the documents.

He kept reading to himself while the rest of us looked at each other for an interpretation of what he was saying.

"Look, dude, we all know you are thmart, but you are going to have to dumb that down a whole lot 'cauth I underthood like two wordth of that," Carl said, still spooning peanut butter into his mouth. "I'm pretty thure Bucket underthood that better than I did."

I'd always thought I was fairly smart, but Sam made me feel like I needed to go back to school starting in fifth grade.

"Basically, in layman's terms, it is saying that they are using these chips to sort of upload information, erase memory, and change behavior. They could literally and completely change a person from thousands of miles away."

"How is that even possible?" Audrey asked.

"Well, until now, I didn't think it was. I mean, the theory behind it has been out there for a while. It looks like Scott's dad's company figured it out a few years before he disappeared. There are emails and receipts that show they were working directly with The United World Federation on this and several other projects. Unfortunately, it doesn't stop there. It continues to get way worse."

"How could it possibly be worse than a possible Gabby Gabe Zombie invasion?" Gabby Gabe had been the one to mandate the chips, and I was horrified that my dad's company had helped him do it. I suspected my dad had been in over his head before he had realized what the company had done. He must have shared the information with my mom and then set a plan for me to find it.

Sam picked up another document. "Oy vey, this file has plans for those that refuse to get the implant. The United World Federation wants to arrest them and even put them to death by decapitating them so companies like Killian Tech and another company called Abendroth Medical Advances can harvest their organs and tissue for medical purposes or research. This is mishigas! They take the brain matter for other studies and experimentation. One study is done before they are even put to death and involves studying the brain patterns in submissive adults and comparing them to those that show opposition. Oof, I guess if you refuse the mark, you're stubborn, and apparently, that is good enough reason for a lobotomy these days."

"WHAT? You mean, they are going to chop my head off because I didn't get a stupid chip? Oh, heck nah, they've gone too far." Carl was pacing around the room and grabbed his throat as if to make sure his head was still attached.

"I am so glad I decided to wait to get the chip until I could research it better. The last thing I want is someone inside my head." Audrey looked like she was shivering even though the temperature inside the storage unit was probably close to ninety degrees.

"Until they chop your head off and then get inside of it," Carl reminded her.

"Look, right now, it is only mandatory in order to work and make purchases," I said, trying to calm everyone down. "No one has said anything about having to get it or else you get your head chopped off. This was probably some scientist that just wanted to use people for research purposes only after they died. Right, Sam?" I was asking him to reassure everyone, but I also wanted to know if he agreed with me. Sam's face was blank. "Right, Sam?" I asked again.

"The ten-year plan's first stage is allowing people to volunteer for the chip, and the next stage is making it mandatory in order to keep working a normal job. After that, well, it looks like it gets a lot worse. Their plans are all ahead of schedule, too." Sam sounded defeated. "And there is more. These other documents are all about biotechnology, genetic engineering, and the transference of the mind's consciousness. I don't like where this is going."

The four of us stood in silence. This was a lot to take in and the last thing I had expected to find.

"There are probably a lot of powerful people who don't want this information out in the world," I said, breaking the silence. "Someone knew my mom had it, and my mom left it for me to find for a reason, so telling the world is exactly what I am going to do." I planned on doing it alone, but Sam stuck his hand into the middle of us.

"You can count me in to help."

Carl's and Audrey's hands followed suit.

"Me, too."

"Me, too."

Chapter Eight

The drive back to Franklin felt surreal. Mila had responded to Sam's earlier text message with, *ok boys enjoy the movie and be safe, and head home when you can*, so we decided to head over to Sam's house, inferring it would be safe there.

We'd left most of the supplies and food in the storage unit. I'd figured it would be easier to go back there to get it rather than take it and store it at my house where I already had access to a lot of the same things. We had gone through every box and every document while we'd been there, and by the time we got to Sam's, it was too late to bother having Max meet up with us. We could catch up with him in the morning.

The lights were on in the house when we pulled up, and we could see Mila pacing in front of the dining room window. When she saw the headlights, she ran to the door to greet us.

Sam ran up to her. "We have a lot to tell you and Dad."

She wrapped him in a big hug before he could say anything else. "Okay, but first you all should head back to the living room. There is something I think you all should see," Mila replied as she let go of Sam. "And, Audrey, it is so nice to see you again." Mila looked at me with an approving yet accusatory grin, and I averted my gaze to save face.

"This is Inspector Bucket. He gave us a hand today. His owners disappeared a while back, and I thought maybe he would like to hang out with us for a while," I said.

Mila bent down and started loving on Bucket. In return, Bucket gave her lots of licks. "Oh, you are a sweetie, aren't you? Of course, you can stay with us for as long as you like!"

We all went inside to the living room, where Joe was watching television. His eyes were fixed so hard on the screen, I didn't think he noticed when we walked into the room.

"Dad…Dad…Abba!"

Joe finally turned to look at us. "Sorry, son, sit down, something big happened today." Joe's demeanor was sad and distant, and we found out why when he turned up the volume on the Global News Broadcast.

"Reporting live from Jerusalem, today we have confirmation that the two men that have been terrorizing anyone who oppose them, who have spoken out against the works of our leader Gabriel Friedman, the men nicknamed the Doomsday Duo, are now reported to be gone for good. In just a few short moments, our cherished leader Mr. Friedman will address the globe. Here with us now is the leader of the United One Global Church." The camera cut from the news anchor to a man standing at an outdoor podium.

"This guy has to be the false prophet, kids," Joe said, keeping his eyes on the television.

"We come to you this morning with discomforting news. The two men who were responsible for many deaths and preaching lies on our streets and who could only be stopped and killed by our beloved Gabriel Friedman were performing an elaborate prank. We saw here earlier today the bodies of those two men who were thought to be dead in the street get up and walk before disappearing. We now believe a secret zealot group is responsible for this prank. I know many of you were in fear when you saw their bodies resurrect on the street, but do not fear! Mr. Friedman himself assures us that it was the work of trickery and that he and only he has power over death. He will be entering the temple this morning to end all further sacrifices, as the Jews have made known their ties with these two men. He will be making the final sacrifice, which will be made to him and him alone!"

Joe hit his hands on the coffee table, and Mila went to comfort him. "We knew this day would come soon. All we can do now is pray and continue to do God's will in all this."

"It's disgusting!" Joe cried out. "I knew that he would end all sacrifices in the temple."

On television, the crowd started screaming and cheering as Gabby Gabe walked up to the podium, replacing the man who'd made the previous announcement. Gabby Gabe's hands went up in the air to quiet the crowd, which only grew louder and began chanting his name. His hands stayed up as if he were against the cheering, but the smile across his face grew, as he clearly wanted nothing more than for the crowd to keep screaming his name. Finally, he began to speak.

"Thank you to all those loyal and faithful to your sovereign government. I have come to the temple for you!"

Loud cheers resonated again throughout the streets around the podium. I was surprised so many people were there. It had to be about six in the morning where they were.

He continued, "I know you are hurting, I know you have wounds to heal. I have heard your cries and have placed the burden on myself. In the coming days, we will be announcing plans to provide each and every one of you around the world ways that you can extend your life and be prosperous. As you go about your days and see those who do not honor and worship me in the way I have earned by refusing to get the mark that we have graciously provided at no charge to the people, they must be called out and dealt with! We have had a large number of Jews supporting the two terrorists that have been speaking lies about me even after all I have done for them. This will no longer be tolerated!"

The cheering grew so loud Joe had to turn down the volume.

"Uncle Ben is in Israel. I talked with him a few hours ago, and they are already making plans to flee to the mountains," Joe said, hanging down his head and resting it in his hands.

"What was that about extended life? Is he promising eternal life to people who take the mark?" Mila sounded heartbroken, her gaze upon the laudatory crowd that the news cameras were panning over.

"Mom, there is something that we found that could explain what he is doing." Sam put his hand on his mom's shoulder.

Joe and Mila looked at Sam curiously.

"Scott's mom left him a key to a storage facility," Sam explained. "There were a lot of supplies and food, but more importantly, there were a lot of incriminating documents."

"Documents? From where?" Joe asked, turning off the television and seeming relieved to have something to divert his attention from it. "I cannot keep this on and watch him go into the temple and make a sacrifice to himself. I just can't!"

Sam nodded in understanding. "Most of the documents seemed like they came directly from Killian Tech Innovations, Scott's dad's company. Dad, they talk about using biotechnologies to prolong life indefinitely, but that isn't even the worst part. That mark people have been putting into their forehead is really a means to access the brain. When people choose to take that mark, it may be the last choice they ever make. He may offer extended life, but he is taking everything else away from them."

"We decided we need to warn people," I interrupted. "There are still a lot of people who haven't gotten around to getting the mark yet. Some of them are literally on the verge. There are underground groups, anarchists, political groups, and all sorts of people who opposed it initially but may give in because they don't understand what it actually does. But we also need to be cautious. There are a lot of other documents here with information on what they eventually plan to do to those that refuse to get it, and it isn't pretty."

"Making a video and getting it broadcasted would probably be the only way to reach people at this point, but getting the message spread is going to be hard. I have tried to make things go viral before, and it hasn't worked for me yet," Carl pointed out. "Of course, those were mostly silly prank videos."

"I know a guy that may be able to help with that. He is great with computers and has been known to be able to hack just about anything," Audrey said.

"Okay, let's make the video then!" I was sure I sounded more enthusiastic than I felt. I was nervous that the repercussions of exposing a world leader would basically be the same as signing my death certificate, but I felt I was meant to do this.

"Are you sure you want to do this?" Sam asked. "The moment you make a video and show your face, you will have a target on your back from the largest organization in the world."

"Maybe we can blur his face or put one of those black lines across his eyes and make it sound like he is Darth Vader," Carl suggested.

"Okay, I think together we can make this work," Sam said, nodding to his brother.

Nate went upstairs to his bedroom to grab some equipment. Sam and his dad went over the documents from the storage unit while Mila wrote out a monologue based on the information Sam and Joe relayed to her. Audrey sat on the couch with Carl and talked about ways to spread the video to as many people as possible.

As everyone scrambled to help me, I went to the bathroom, closed the lid on the toilet, sat down, and put my face into my hands. The idea of praying wasn't new to me, but the action certainly was. I didn't know how to start or what to say, so I began by saying how I was feeling. "Oh, God, I'm lost. Like, in every way possible, I'm lost. I know I need You. I just wish I never ignored You before. I'm so sorry for that, sorry for not listening to my mom, sorry for not acknowledging You, sorry for all the lies I've told to get out of going to church, sorry for just everything. I can't even begin to list everything I'm sorry for because it would take me the next eighteen years, I'm sure. I want to start over. I want You in my life this time."

I felt tears running down my cheeks. I stood up, stared at myself in the mirror, and continued to pray. "I am nothing without You, God! And now, all this information that I have been given the last couple days, all that has happened, has happened because of You. You allowed for this information to get out, for us to be able to reach people, but I am not worthy to do this. I don't want anyone else to have to do this, to put themselves in a bad spot. God, help me, help us. I know now that you sent your Son to die for me, and I certainly didn't deserve it, but I will never take it for granted again. Please, God, save me, and save my friends!"

There was a knock on the bathroom door. "Hey, man, are you okay in there?" It was Carl. "We are all ready for you out here. Scott, are you good?"

"Yeah, man, be there in a minute." I blew my nose with a wad of toilet paper then washed my hands and face. I was about to do something crazy, but for the first time in my life, I felt a sense of peace I couldn't explain.

Since I didn't have my phone, we made the video with Carl's. In it, I shared some of the proof and documents from my dad's company. Carl sent a copy of the video to everyone in the room. Audrey texted the friend she thought could help us spread the video and asked if we could meet with him tomorrow.

 Mila insisted we all stay over that night. They had one guest room upstairs, which we gave to Audrey. Carl and I took the two living room couches. Mila made sure we each had sheets, blankets, pillows, and a toothbrush before she went upstairs to her room. Bucket started off on the floor, but it wasn't long before he had crawled up with me on the couch.

"Hey, Scott, you still awake?" Carl asked.

"Yeah, man, what's up?" I was finding it hard to fall asleep even though I was extremely tired.

"I just wanted to let you know that I prayed today and asked Jesus to be my Savior. I want that for you, too, ya know?"

"I prayed tonight, too," I said, sitting up from the couch. Carl sat up with me. "From now on, we aren't just best friends, Carl, we are brothers."

He held out his hand to me, and I grabbed it, pulled him forward, and hugged him.

"Brothers," Carl agreed.

This would be the third night in a row that I didn't get much sleep. My mind couldn't shut off. I kept thinking about Gary, my dad's company, the mark, and Detective Clarke. I would start to pray, and then I would start thinking about everything all over again. There were, like, ten puzzles to solve, but I suspected all of them were connected in some way or another.

Chapter Nine

I woke up Saturday morning to the smell of bacon. It was probably my favorite food outside of Mila's brisket as well as one of my favorite smells. My mom used to make bacon every morning before I went to school, and the smell alone triggered memories of her standing in the kitchen waving her spatula in the air as Dad passed by her swatting her on her backside. I'd always made a face and noise of disgust when he'd done that, but now I missed it.

"All my life, I stayed away from this stuff. I didn't know what I was missing!" Joe said, taking a strip from the plate by the stove and throwing it into his mouth. Mila tried to swat his hand away, but her efforts were in vain, as he was already on his second strip of bacon by the time I stood up. I looked to where Carl had slept, and there lay only a pile of blankets.

Joe reached for more bacon, and Mila smacked his hand.

"I told you, that is Scott's plate, you already had enough!" Mila said as she poked Joe's belly.

Joe threw up his hands in defeat. "Okay, fine, but I am only stopping for Scott. I have no intention of trying to get back my six-pack abs." Joe patted his stomach.

Mila laughed. "You'd be lucky to get rid of those two liters you got there, and I'm pretty sure you never had a six pack!"

Their playful banter reminded me even more of my parents. The difference was that the only time my parents had been like that had been in the mornings before my dad had headed off to work. He would often stay late at the office, and I thought him and Mom always tried to make the best of the time they had together in the morning.

Mila handed me a plate with eggs, toast, and bacon. It looked amazing.

"Thank you! But what about everyone else?" I asked. I looked around the room and didn't see Carl or Bucket.

"They had breakfast a couple hours ago. I thought you might need some sleep, so I didn't want to wake you. I figured if you weren't awake by the time I finished cooking yours, I would let Joe have some of your bacon. I think God woke you up since He knows Joe certainly doesn't need any more." Mila laughed. "You actually got one more piece than everyone else because I knew sticky fingers over here would snag a few!"

Joe shrugged his shoulders. "Guilty as charged."

I laughed and turned my attention to the delicious breakfast Mila had made for me. I didn't realize how hungry I'd been until I was half finished.

Carl, Sam, and Audrey walked in through the back door with Bucket by their side. Sam had a fresh basket of eggs in his hands, and Carl was carrying a pail of milk.

"Well, look who finally decided to join the land of the living. It's the CEO of sleeping in!" Carl joked, taking the pail of milk to the counter to help Mila pour it into glass jars.

"What? Why? What time is it, anyway?" I asked self-consciously.

"It's already after eleven a.m.," Audrey said.

I felt a little embarrassed. I never slept in that late, but yesterday I had overslept as well, and Audrey knew that, too. I hoped she wouldn't think I did this all the time.

"I couldn't sleep last night," I said defensively.

"No one is blaming you," Audrey insisted. "We all wanted you to sleep in. You needed it."

Her reassurance did not make my embarrassment fade, but I did recognize the care my friends were showing toward me and appreciated it.

"By the way, Scott, I helped Mila make yogurt this morning, gathered eggs, and milked the goats, so I will be needing you to call me Farmer Carl for the rest of the day," Carl said with both fists on his hips and his chin lifted.

"Alright, there, Farmer Carl. I guess since you've been getting the eggs in, maybe the cops that were looking for me the other day will start looking for you now instead," I said.

Carl's face turned serious. "Why is that?"

"'Cause they will suspect you of foul play, duh."

"Dude, that is way worse than any of my jokes," Carl said, shaking his head.

"Yeah, well, I know that I heard some snickering coming from the ladies," I replied.

"They're just being nice because you are a nice, cute boy, Scott," Carl said, laughing.

The others laughed along with him, and after a brief second, I laughed as well.

"Sorry to break up your guys' stand-up routines, as awesome as they are, but we probably need to leave soon," Audrey said. "Sam is going to drive us all over to Max's house to pick him up, and then we are going to head over to my friend Russell's house to see if he can help us do something with the video."

"Can he be trusted?" I asked with my mouth full of eggs.

"I mean, he hates most forms of government, and he hates the current world leaders and organizations more than anything else. He also doesn't like it when people have their privacy invaded, so I think he will be more than happy to help us and be discreet about it. Besides, I think he is our best shot at getting this thing out there even if he couldn't be fully trusted," Audrey reassured me.

"Well, that sounds like an ally in my book," Carl exclaimed.

"We will have to leave Inspector Bucket here. We won't have room for him in the car," I said, bending over to pet him. He dropped to the floor and rolled on his back so I could rub his belly.

"Well, I look forward to Inspector Bucket's company today," Mila said.

We all took turns taking showers and getting dressed in new clothes. I hated to admit to anyone that it had been a few days since I'd showered. Between oversleeping every day and running from people at night, hygiene had been in the back of my mind. I threw on a shirt that said, "Don't trust atoms, they make up everything." Sam and I were roughly the same size, but we had very different styles and taste in clothes. Mila had some pants and shirts for Audrey to wear, and Carl was able to at least change his shirt into one of Nick's.

We all got into Sam's car and drove to Max's house, and when we pulled up to it, I slid to the middle seat in the back closer to Audrey. I put my hands together and sat them in my lap, self-conscious about touching Audrey and making her uncomfortable. My shoulder bumped hers as Max slid into the seat I'd vacated, and I apologized because I didn't know how to act all of a sudden.

"So, what did I miss?" Max was clearly happy to be part of the group again.

"Only everything," Sam replied.

"I could tell you, but then I'd have to kill you," Carl said in his deepest voice.

Max glanced at Audrey in an odd fashion, as if he were judging her. She looked ahead.

"Well, it all started with the bus stop," I said, trying to break the tension. I told him everything that had happened, including everything we'd found in the documents. Max listened in silence until the part about the documents, which he surprisingly seemed interested in. He wanted to know more about them and where the storage unit was. I was telling him about all the other stuff we had found in the unit when I looked up and saw a bus pulling into the bus station on the opposite side of the street.

Gary was driving the bus.

"Hey, pull over! I need to jump out for a second!" I shouted.

Sam quickly pulled to the curb, and Max jumped out of the car to let me out. I ran across the street just before Gary closed his doors.

"Hey, man! I was worried about you! Some guy was driving your route yesterday and said you didn't work for the bus company anymore. You had me all kinds of worried!"

Gary looked confused and said, "Sorry, son, I think you have the wrong person."

"It's me, Scott! Don't mess with me, Gary, I was freaking out yesterday."

"I mean, my name is Gary, but I don't recall meeting you, so my apologies. Are you riding with us today? We really need to get going, sir," Gary replied, wiping the sweat from his brow while lifting the lid of his hat off his head.

I could see the mark clear as day. I knew he'd only had the mark on his hand as of yesterday morning, and it broke my heart that he no longer knew who I was. For a brief moment, I'd thought he was pretending not to know me so that he wouldn't get in trouble again, but it was clear he was no longer the same Gary that I'd known.

"Sorry, sir, I think I mixed you up with one of the other drivers. You, uh, have a good day," I said as I stepped back from the bus. I waved at Gary one last time through the closing bus doors. There was a huge knot in my throat. I felt like I had found out my favorite uncle had died. Gary had been a huge part of my life for the last three years. My sadness quickly turned to anger, and I ran back to the car.

"He didn't even know who I was. It was like he had no memory of me at all," I said as I slid back in the car. Audrey put her hand on my back, and I felt immediate comfort.

"I'm sorry, I know how worried you were about him. I wish it would have turned out better, but this is a good reason to find Russell and get his help as soon as we can."

Sam waited for the bus to pull away before pulling back onto the road and driving forward. Gary didn't even look the same. His normal smiling face looked cold and distant as he drove away.

"Okay, go past the courthouse and turn right on Main Street at the light," Audrey said.

"Got it," Sam nodded as he looked at us in the rearview mirror.

The courthouse was only two blocks away, but we could already hear people chanting, "Give us back our freedoms!" Their voices echoed in the streets, and as we approached, we saw people holding signs and posters with different sayings about freedom, government control, and government overreach. I wasn't sure protesting would matter since all local governments had been taken over by the federal government, and the federal government just reiterated what the United World Federation stated.

They were protesting things that were much bigger than anything Franklin, Indiana, could affect, but at least the protests were proof that not everyone was on board with the United World Federation's decrees. They would never be able to get everyone to comply.

We slowed down as we passed the rioters. There were vans out front from *Channel 4 News* and some local radio stations. In the center of it all stood a man in his twenties. He was overweight and wore an oversized yellow t-shirt. He had unkempt brown hair that hung to his collar, large glasses, and a full beard. He looked angry at the world as he shouted, "Give us back our freedoms!" He was someone I definitely wouldn't want to tick off.

"Hey, there's Russell, right there," Audrey said, pointing at the same man I had been staring at.

"Oh, boy," I said, unsure I still wanted to talk to him. Russell was a little intimidating, but Audrey seemed confident that he could help us.

We all stepped out of the car and walked toward the protestors. I wasn't sure this was the best time to reach out to Russell, but time wasn't something we could waste. Someone from *Channel 4 News* pulled Russell aside to get a one-on-one interview with him before we could talk to him, so we stepped aside and waited while Russell went on a rant about Gabby Gabe.

"He comes at us with promises while taking over powers and diminishing our freedoms! We used to be a proud nation that held to the belief that freedom was a right, that no man had to bow to another or curtail their beliefs in order to escape tyranny! Our once-beloved democracy has turned into a despotism controlled by a man who only seeks more control and more power every day. Our choices are being stripped away! Our freedoms are being obliterated before our eyes! But the world's eyes are shut! He entertains you with sideshows claiming his powers come from a god with his left hand while his right hand annihilates our people. He has dissolved our ability to come up with our own solutions and our own prerogatives! We can no longer stand idly by and allow him to force himself upon us! If we come together and reject his 'mark,' he cannot come after all of us! Today, we make known our insurgence!"

Russell threw his right fist into the air, and the crowd cheered. At the same time, coming toward the crowds and news crew were several officers that did not look very happy with Russell's motivational speech. One of the officers pulled the plug from the camera that was filming while others headed toward Russell. Russell slipped back into the crowd and threw on a black baseball cap and black jacket.

"I have an idea," I said. "Audrey, you and Sam get Russell. Get him safe and out of here. Drive him over to Audrey's house while Max, Carl, and I head there on foot. I have a feeling if we don't get this guy out of here, the police will."

Audrey and Sam both nodded and took off in opposite directions as if they had planned this ahead of time. Sam retrieved the car, and Audrey went to grab Russell. He didn't hesitate to follow Audrey's lead when she came up beside him, put her arm in his, and led him toward the car. The rest of us waited until we saw them get into the car and drive off then looked around to see if anyone had noticed. The officers were walking around the crowd, looking at the face of each person they passed. They must not have seen Russell leave with Audrey.

The three of us started walking, and as we walked by the news crew, I heard a man yelling at the journalist who had interviewed Russell. "Why would you air that over live TV? You could've predicted what he would say, and now I am going to get my butt handed to me for letting him speak and not stopping it from going live! What were you thinking?"

We kept walking with our heads down. I wasn't sure if I was still a person of interest to these guys, but as far as I could tell, none of the officers looked familiar or were the ones that had been at my house.

After we passed the crowd and patrol cars, I breathed a sigh of relief. It was a beautiful day, and I realized it had been a while since I had just appreciated the things around me. A warm breeze was chased by the sounds of birds chirping. The walk to Audrey's house was a change from all the running and sneaking around I had been doing lately.

As we were passing the shop where I had met Audrey, Carl pushed my arm. "What is up with that big grin on your face? It looks like you just opened up a love letter or something."

I felt like he and Max could see into my thoughts, and I was completely embarrassed. "I was just enjoying the nice walk for a change," I said, hoping they didn't realize I had been daydreaming about Audrey as well. I hadn't realized how much I liked her until now.

"Well, we just passed the place where you met Audrey, and then that big stupid smile popped on your face, so I'm pretty sure it isn't the weather you are smiling about." At first, Max sounded more annoyed than amused, but then he started to laugh. "You guys were so into each other that day, you both left me at the shop. You didn't even say goodbye."

Carl put his hand up to his mouth as if to cough but instead started to laugh. "Oh, dog, you totally ditched Max for a girl! That's great!"

I hadn't realized we had left Max without saying goodbye until this moment. "Sorry, man. At first, I was upset about not getting the job. I had overslept that morning, and I was all frazzled. I just didn't think. For real, I'm sorry."

"Ah, no worries. To be honest, I didn't even realize you were both gone until the end of the day anyway," Max said, pushing me in the back. "I was just more bummed I didn't get to go with you to the storage unit. I was bored, and my mom made spinach for dinner, which I hate."

We passed the bus stop where I had first found out that something had happened to Gary. My expression quickly turned somber as I gazed toward the street. "I wish I never walked onto that bus that morning. If I hadn't woken up late and had ridden my bike like I originally planned, Gary would still be Gary."

"You can't blame yourself, man. You don't know that! You just gotta keep going forward and try to help others. We have to change our focus from what has happened to what we are going to do next, and hopefully that Russell dude can help us do that." Carl seemed like an adult all of a sudden.

I reached up and grabbed his shoulder. "Together," I said.

"Together," Carl repeated.

Chapter Ten

We couldn't see Sam's car as we approached Audrey's house, and a sinking feeling fell over me. Leaving Carl and Max, I picked up the pace until I was running up to the house, where I noticed the tire tracks in the side yard leading to the back. I ran behind the house next to the fence line and saw Sam's car parked in the backyard. *Thank you, God.*

I ran back to the front and motioned for Max and Carl to come around back to avoid drawing suspicion if anyone was watching. Max and Carl were still a few houses back and ducked behind the house a few doors down to come toward Audrey's house from the back.

We knocked on the back door, and a few moments later, Audrey appeared behind the window curtain.

"You guys made it!" When she opened the door, Audrey looked like she was about to reach out to hug me, but she patted my shoulder instead before walking back to the living room.

Russell was sitting on the couch looking over the papers Sam had taken from the storage unit. He appeared to be concentrating deeply, so I didn't want to interrupt, but I didn't want to let the moment pass by either.

I stuck out my hand. "Scott Killian, nice to meet you."

"Russell Polansheki. I know, it's a mouthful."

"We need your help," I said. "We want to get this message out to as many people as possible via video. Audrey thought you may be able to help us hack into the government's websites and post this information there or maybe even hack into the news media and post the video live on TV."

"Look, kid." Russell calling me *kid* felt weird since he was probably only about five years older than me. He shook his head, and I could tell he was calling me an idiot silently in his thoughts. "Back in 2020, the Russians were going all cyber-attack crazy, breaking into all sorts of government organizations. The government has been increasing its cybersecurity ever since. Now, it's true, on the flip side, cybercriminals are constantly developing new ways to combat the newer security measures, but it's not easy. Now, I'm not saying I can't do it, but it is a whole lot of work for basically nothing."

"What do you mean, for nothing?" I knew I sounded deflated as the words came out of my mouth.

"I mean just that. If I could get into their web pages and post this information, the only people who would read it would be the people who work for the government. Before anyone else could view it, it would be taken down. Not to mention, I don't need to give the Department of Homeland Security another reason to come after me. The same goes for the local news channels. They are a dying news source. You would have a few local people watching these channels live. No doubt, the channels would end the broadcast before the entire video could be seen."

Russell paced in a small circle. "No. I have a much better idea. I can take this video Sam told me all about in the car and hack, like, the top twenty accounts held by influencers, and post it there. From there, it should spread like wildfire. The faster the influencers take them down, the faster people will share it because people will want to see what video was removed from their favorite accounts. It will be good if it is known as a banned video. It will pique enough curiosity that it will be searched for even when people can't find it anymore. Just one of these so-called influencers could have a huge following. Do this with several accounts from several countries and genres, and this video should be seen by millions. It's too late to stop this power-hungry jerk, but it may be enough to slow him down and give the people an idea into what he is doing. I knew he was horrible, but I never knew it was this bad."

"I'll give you one," Carl said overconfidently. "You can post it on my account. I'm the man. I have, like, four thousand followers!"

Russell shook his head, grinning. "That's great, bud, I'm really proud of you and all, but the accounts I'm aiming for have an upward of five hundred million followers."

Carl looked at Russell with a straight face. "Man, why you gotta knock me down like that?"

The rest of us laughed.

"My apologies," Russell said, still laughing. "We will for sure share it on your account as well."

"That's what I'm talking about!" Carl threw a punch into the air as if he had just been confirmed as "the man."

"Just give me your username, account password, mother's maiden name, and social security number," Russell said as he winked and smiled.

Carl's grin vanished. "Okay, that's not fair."

"So can you do it? Can you legit hack these large accounts?" I asked, now feeling both excited and nervous.

Russell nodded. "Give me a couple of days, but I do want to be a part of this. Nothing makes me happier than to see government authority come crumbling down. Oh, and I appreciate you guys getting me out of there today. I think I may have already pushed some buttons. Sometimes a small voice can spread far, but at this point, I think I'm just ticking off the local authorities, and I'm okay with that."

"Sam and I can take you home when you are ready," Max said.

Max's initiative surprised me. He wasn't normally the type to offer help or make decisions in the group. Most of the time, he seemed to be just along for the ride. Maybe he had been feeling so left out the last couple of days he felt the need to insert himself into what we were doing. I started to worry I hadn't been a good friend. I knew that Max wasn't on board with the idea that the rapture was the cause of the disappearances and that his friends were all changing before his eyes, but he still wanted to be a part of what we were doing.

"Before you go, I wanted to show you something else," Audrey said. She went to the dining room table and grabbed her Bible. "I know you are agnostic, but I thought you may find this interesting." She glanced at Max as if to include him in the conversation. "So I want to read you this passage in the book of Revelation. In Chapter 13:16-17, it says, 'And he causes all, the small and the great, the rich and the poor, and the free and the slaves, to be given a mark on their right hands or their foreheads, and he decrees that no one will be able to buy or to sell, except the one who has the mark, either the name of the beast or the number of his name.' I—uh, rather, *we*—believe that Gabriel is this man, and that this time is here."

Russell sat with his mouth twisted to the side before breaking the silence. "The verse is compelling to describe what is currently happening, but where does that leave us? It means fighting this is pointless, and that war and death are inevitable."

"Fighting it means fewer people will succumb to the deception this guy is feeding us." Sam always seemed to know how to answer tough questions. "It means there is hope for those that reject him. Rejecting him isn't enough though, so we are also fighting for truth, and we believe the truth is that Jesus was, or I should say *is,* the Son of God who died for us."

"I understand why you want to fight this, I do," Russell replied. "I really do. I think I need to look at this on my own time in my own space so I can come at this with both logic and an open mind. I do appreciate you guys fighting this in your own way, though. I promise I will give this some thought, and I don't mind the trouble, either. I rather welcome it."

"Trouble is an understatement," I began. "My house has been broken into, we were followed, and we were chased by a car, and I feel like I'm sugarcoating it."

"Well, I've said this before, I prefer dangerous freedom over peaceful slavery any day. Oh, and I could use a little real excitement in my life from time to time."

"Oh, I like the way that sounds," Carl said as he put his right hand up in the air and made a sliding motion as if writing the words on a giant billboard. "Dangerous freedom!"

Russell laughed. "Yeah, some of my friends have been saying that for years. Never thought it would get like this, though. You guys are alright in my book. Do any of you like to play board games or card games? Usually, games are where I get all my social interactions and entertainment."

"Sometimes," Max replied. "I think I just have to be in the mood, I guess."

"I've always been more of a video-game person," I added.

"I'm probably the odd one out because I prefer solitary puzzles like crypto quips," Sam said.

"I also love video games and crypto quips as well. I pretty much like any game or puzzle in any form," Russell said. "I wouldn't mind hanging out with you all sometime. This world is getting lonelier and lonelier. People who I thought would never jump on the bandwagon are now practically ambassadors for the stupid chip. I just don't get it. I guess if we don't get chased down by real cars, maybe we can chase each other down in the new Turbo Charge game that just came out."

Russell stood up while he was speaking, but before he could take a step forward, he fell back into his seat. As the room shook violently, we all grasped onto something or someone close. The refrigerator door flew open, some of the lights flickered, and dishes rattled in the kitchen, a few of them falling to the ground with a smash. It was a good thing we were at Audrey's house since she didn't have much inside of her house that could cause anyone harm. Carl had his arms stretched out and braced himself between the open doorway between the living room and kitchen. His eyes were still shut even after the earthquake had stopped. Audrey stood next to me and had her arms wrapped tight around mine. Sam had stayed on the couch but had bent over with his head down and his hands covering his head, and Max had gotten himself down on the floor.

"Maybe it's a sign," Russell said as he laughed.

"Yeah, but a sign for what?" Max responded.

Carl opened one eye while still bracing himself against the doorframe, hesitant to move, but his one eye did see Audrey's arm wrapped around mine. "Does she make the earth move for ya, Scott?" Carl snickered.

Audrey quickly let go of my arm and looked down.

"You're a dream, Scotty," Carl said, batting his eyelashes.

"Yeah, well, go back to sleep then, Carl!" I said as I turned to Audrey, put up my hands, and shrugged my shoulders. She smiled back then turned her head as she blushed.

Sam and Max were both laughing. I wasn't quite sure if they were laughing at me, at Carl, or at both of us.

"I think we should get going then since things seem settled down," Sam said. I thought he was trying to save me from further embarrassment.

"Okay, so the plan is Sam and Max will take Russell home and then swing back by here and get the rest of us. I think we should drive by my house and see if they still have police surveillance there, and if not, we can grab some supplies and bring them over to Sam's house. After all that. we should definitely eat, 'cause I am already hungry even though I had that huge breakfast at Sam's!"

Everyone agreed, and Audrey went out to open the gate so Sam could pull out his car. Carl and I sat on the couch as everyone was leaving.

"Hey, man, I was just kidding around earlier. Hope I didn't embarrass you too much. I mean, I hope I embarrassed you, for sure, but just not too much." Carl laughed and slapped me on the back.

"Yeah," I said, chuckling. "It's all good. It kind of helped me out a little. I kind of like her and want her to know but don't know how to tell her, so I guess you did the hard work for me."

"I knew it!" Carl said proudly.

"Yeah, I don't think it was a big mystery there. Inspector Bucket could have solved this riddle," I retorted. "Maybe your new name is now Inspector Farmer Carl."

Audrey came back in, and Carl slapped me on the back again before standing up to allow Audrey to sit on the couch next to me. It was silent for what seemed like an eternity. Carl kept looking at me and smiling and wiggling his eyebrows up and down. I would look over at Audrey to see if she noticed, and she would look at me, and then I would turn my head away, embarrassed. This cycle went on several times while I tried to think of something to talk about.

"So," I finally said, "is this the type of stuff you normally do on a Saturday when you are off work?" I meant to ask it as a joke, but it came out sounding as if I were being serious.

Carl looked at me, wincing, then rubbed his forehead and laughed a little behind his hand. I was failing to make small talk on every level.

"Do you trust your friends?" Audrey asked out of nowhere.

"Uh, yeah, sure. Why?" I was thrown off by the question.

"I don't know. I was just thinking about everything and about the guy that had been following you, and I just feel like something doesn't quite make sense about it," Audrey said.

"Like what?" I asked.

"I don't know. I guess I was just thinking about how the guy following you knew where you were all the time, and it seemed a little odd. Like, I know you said you left your phone at Carl's because you thought maybe you were being tracked, but if the guy wasn't working with the cops, then do you honestly think some random guy would be able to trace your phone? I think maybe you are a little too trusting."

"Too trusting? What do you mean? You are the one that had me give a copy of the video we made to someone who was practically a stranger and then let two of my friends leave with him." My voice grew louder as I talked.

"Look, I'm sorry I mentioned it, but you barely know me. We met less than a week ago, and you have trusted me with all this information, and I just think that if you trusted someone else with all of it, then it could put us all in a bad spot. I mean, how do you know I didn't call someone to tell them your plans and to tell them where to find your storage unit or anything else?"

Carl's jaw had dropped, and his eyes were wide open. Instead of processing what Audrey was saying and trying to make sense of the possibility of being betrayed, I grew defensive.

"Well, I am sorry I thought I could trust you! I thought we connected in a few areas, and when you helped me, I felt I could open up to you. Guess I was wrong." I stood up and briskly walked to the back door, opened it, and slammed it behind me. Standing on the concrete slab outside, I quickly regretted storming out. I felt stupid and childish. I was still a little angry and hurt, though, and I didn't want to walk back in and try to make things right, either.

It was only a moment before the back door opened behind me. Carl stood with a shocked look on his face. "Dude, I don't think she meant anything bad. I think she just felt something was off and was trying to figure things out."

Carl's words made me feel more childish and stupid. Why had I reacted like that?

"I've known you for a long time, man," Carl continued, "and I have never seen you act like that before. You must have it bad. Like, real bad!"

I closed my eyes and hung my head. "Yeah, well, doesn't matter now anyway 'cause I completely blew it."

"I don't know, man, she seemed more upset with herself than she was at you when you stormed off like a toddler."

I darted a look at Carl. "Gee, thanks for coming out here and making me feel better."

"Hey, man, that's what friends are for," Carl said. "Now I'm going to help you fix this, and when I do, you can call me Matchmaker, Inspector, Farmer Carl." Carl laughed.

"Not amused," I said. I slapped him on the back and started to go back into the house, but before we could walk in, we heard Sam's car pulling back up.

<u>Chapter Eleven</u>

The ride over to my house was super quiet. Sam kept looking at me through the rearview mirror as if to ask me what was wrong. At least Audrey had come with us. There had been a brief moment when I'd thought she wasn't going to come, but Carl had convinced her.

This time, Max was in the front, and Carl sat in the back in the middle. His long legs looked like they were pushing his knees up to his face. Luckily, the drive to my house did not take long, and when we arrived, there wasn't any police presence in sight.

I felt a tinge of nervousness walking up to the house. I had never felt afraid in my own house, even when I was alone, but with recent events, I no longer trusted the place I called home. We walked in, and the house looked untouched from the last time I had been there.

I went to the kitchen, grabbed a Coke from the fridge, and began chugging it without closing the refrigerator door. I stopped when I heard Carl loudly clearing his throat.

"Ahem."

"Oh! Sorry, guys!" Everyone was standing in the doorway of the kitchen staring at me. "Who wants a Coke?" I started passing cans around to everyone. "Sorry, but I have been dying for a soda!"

"The world is coming to an end, and you are just dying for a soda," Carl said flatly.

"Okay, maybe I exaggerated that a bit," I said, laughing. "On the other hand, now that I have downed an entire Coke in less than a minute, I think my mind is clearing up and I can think better now."

"Maybe soda companies can start using that as their marketing ploy," Sam chuckled. "They can offer their services to schools for test time."

"It worked for me in high school," I said as I raised my can high into the air.

"Your definition of 'worked' is vastly different from my definition of 'worked'. Tachles, you scraped by most of your classes, and most of your Bs probably should have been Cs. Maybe drink a few more so you can remember that properly," Sam joked.

"I could have been drinking straight fish oil in high school and I wouldn't have had straight As in all honors classes like you had," I replied.

"Oh, that is very true. I can definitely testify to that," Carl said. "Of course, I think Sam had a D minus in people skills and most definitely an F in talking to women, even when I tried tutoring him."

Sam punched Carl in the arm, and the rest of us laughed, including Audrey, which made me feel better since she had been so quiet and somber during our ride over here.

"On a more serious note, though, I couldn't help but wonder why my parents went to the trouble of hiding that information from me for so long.

It was obvious they wanted me to know what was going on in the company, so why not just tell me? Why hide the evidence away from the house?" I asked as I grabbed food and supplies out of the cabinets.

"Maybe they thought you might not be in the house to find it if you were taken away after they disappeared," Max suggested.

"Yeah, but that doesn't make sense either. I would have had to find the key to the storage unit here, so either way, I would have had to have access to the house," I replied, puzzled. "You guys look around in the pantry and laundry room for food and supplies to pack up and bring to Sam's house. Sam and I are going to go upstairs and look around in my parents' room to see if we can come across anything else."

"I'll come up with you guys," Max suggested.

"No, that's okay, I think there are more hands needed down here to help get everything loaded into the trunk," I said. I thought maybe he didn't want to be grouped with Audrey since they didn't seem to get along that well but figured they were both adults and could get along for fifteen minutes or so.

Sam and I went up the stairs, and as we passed by my room, Sam looked in and saw the teddy bear on the floor with his head torn off and stuffing ripped out. "Is that where you found the key to the storage unit, or were you just taking some heated animosity out on old Teddy there?" Sam asked.

I had forgotten I hadn't told him exactly what had happened. "No, actually, funny story, I arrived home from the police station that night, and someone had been here looking for something and took the head off poor Teddy thinking he was the Ted in the letter."

Sam froze. "Wait, someone came here after we read the letter to look for the key to the storage unit? How? I mean, how could anyone know where to look or have gotten those clues? Scott, this could be bad."

"I know. I've been trying to be extra cautious. I don't carry my phone on me anymore and—"

"No wonder your mom's letter was so weird and cryptic. I thought it was odd she didn't just tell you where stuff was. She must have known someone would be after it. This also sounds like someone betrayed you, achi! I mean, I'm sorry, but unfortunately, that's how it sounds. Did you tell anyone else about the letter besides who was in the police station?"

"Only Audrey, but that was after the fact. Like, after the person was here searching for the key," I replied. "But then when Detective Clarke showed up at her house—"

"Wait, what?" Sam shouted.

"I forgot I didn't mention that part to you. Everything has been happening so fast. I mentioned it earlier to Carl and forgot you weren't there when I told him."

Sam became quiet. He went into my parents' room and started looking through stuff, and I helped him search. Everything in their room had been untouched since they had disappeared. I always felt sad coming in here, so I avoided it as much as possible.

After about twenty minutes of searching and not finding anything, Sam sat down on the bed. "I can't help but feel like we are missing something," he said.

"I've been saying that myself," I replied. "I'm going to run downstairs real quick and check on the others. I'll be right back."

Downstairs, it looked like my friends had emptied the entire contents of my cabinets onto the counters. Carl and Audrey had just walked back in from outside, and Max was eating a can of ravioli.

"I figured I would save the effort of packing this can and eat it now," he said with a grin.

"Ha, yeah, that's fine! If you like that, then I would be happy to cook for you anytime. It's one of my specialties."

"I'm sure," Max said, laughing, "but sadly, it is better than my mom's cooking."

"Most of the hatchback is full. We only have room for a couple more items as long as they are small. Do you want to take a trip with Sam to drop this off and then come back and we can pack up some more?" Audrey asked.

"Yeah, I'll go get Sam. I think I may wait here just in case the cops that were here watching the house come by again. This way they won't arrest you guys thinking you are strangers in my house."

When I returned upstairs to get Sam, he was still sitting on the edge of the bed looking at the wall. "Hey, man, was wondering if you wanted to take a trip to your parents' with some of these supplies."

"Uh, yeah. Sounds good. I'll be down in a minute." Sam sounded deep in thought, so I went back downstairs without him, where I found Audrey in the kitchen alone.

"Hey," I said, unsure how to apologize to her but knowing I had to try. "I'm sorry I blew up on you earlier. I think I just need to admit that I'm in over my head, and it's my fault that I am."

"Scott, it is not your fault that you are in this situation. There are some bad men out there doing bad things, and it is their fault that you are feeling like you are over your head," Audrey said as she reached for my hand. "And you aren't alone, and I'm sorry I made you feel that way."

As soon as Carl and Max walked back into the house, Audrey let go of my hand, but not before they both saw. Carl mimicked Audrey and grabbed Max's hand. They both turned to each other.

"I'm so sorry, smoochy pooh. You are the prettiest little Maxie-pooh in the world," Carl said in a high-pitched voice.

"Thank you, Carl-pooh, you are the strongest, most heroic man I know," Max joined in with Carl's buffoonery.

"No wonder the ladies are just falling all over you two guys," Audrey retorted. "Who can resist such maturity?"

Carl and Max both laughed so hard it was obvious Audrey's sarcasm had no effect on them.

"Which one of you bozos wants to go with Sam to help him, and which one of you wants to stay here and help us?" I asked.

They both looked at each other, shrugged, then played "rock, paper, scissors." Carl won and threw up his hands in victory.

"So what did you win? Staying or going?" I asked.

"Oh! We never actually decided that part," Carl stammered.

"Idiots," Audrey mumbled.

"Do you want to help Sam? I can help out here," Max suggested.

"Okay, sounds good to me," Carl said, heading out the door. Sam was already coming down the stairs when Carl walked out, and Sam walked out behind him to the car without saying goodbye to anyone.

"Is he okay?" Audrey asked.

"Yeah, I think he is just lost in his head right now. He gets that way sometimes when he is deep in thought."

"So does Mrs. Stern want these cans of ravioli, or is it cool if I pack some of these up to bring to my house?" Max asked, eating another can.

"There is a box right over there if you want to run some over to your house," I said, "but you may want to hide it from your mom. You may offend her since I know she likes to cook all your dinners when you are home."

"Truth," Max said, pointing his finger at me.

It didn't seem like much time had passed before Carl and Sam came back.

"That was quick," I said as Sam walked past us again and up the stairs.

"Yeah, Nate was there, and he and Joe helped us carry everything in the house as Mila put everything away. She said to give you this," Carl said and then engulfed me in his long arms.

"Gee, thanks for the hug, bud," I said.

"Don't thank me. That hug came directly from Mrs. S.," Carl replied.

"Remind me later to let her know that sending hugs won't be necessary," I said.

"Hey! My hugs are premium hugs, and you were lucky to get one, sir."

"Okay, but they lose value the more you give out, so just keep that in mind," I yelled back as I walked up the stairs to check on Sam.

Sam was sitting on the bed again, his glasses lying on the bed next to him. His hair was sticking up more than usual, I assumed from rubbing his hands through his hair while he was thinking. I thought about turning around and going back downstairs when he started to talk.

"Someone was following you. Why?"

"Because they found out my parents left me something?"

"Yes, he knew you had the information somewhere about your dad's company. So why isn't he here now? He knew where you lived. He could have been watching the house and knew you returned." Sam was talking to me, but it sounded more like he was talking to himself.

"Ummmm because he, uh, knows it's too late? I already found the information, so he doesn't have to stop me from finding it now?"

"Why didn't he want you to have it?"

"He didn't want me to share it?"

The moment the words came out of my mouth, Sam and I turned to look at each other and simultaneously yelled, "RUSSELL!"

Sam jumped up from the bed, and we both ran down the stairs. We ran out the door and into Sam's car. As Sam backed out of the driveway, I looked out the passenger window to see Carl and Audrey standing at the doorway we'd left open, Carl's hands up in the air. Sam whipped the car around the corner toward Russell's house.

"I know we are in a hurry, but slow down. I don't want us to draw attention to ourselves," I said.

"I just have a bad feeling about this," Sam replied.

Sam kept the same pace, and I looked behind us as he drove to make sure no one followed us. Sam turned onto a side street, and as he straightened out the steering wheel, a car zipped by us heading in the opposite direction. Both our heads whipped around to follow the car.

"Dude, is that the same car that followed us before?" Sam asked.

I felt positive it was the same car that had chased us earlier this week. My heart started to race. It looked like it had left the same place we were heading.

Sam whipped into the driveway at Russell's house. We both jumped out of the car and ran to the door. Sam beat me to the porch and started pounding on the front door. We didn't hear anything from inside the house, so Sam tried the door. It was open. We burst through the front door and started running through the house calling out his name. "RUSSELL! RUSSELL! You here, man?"

I made my way to the back hallway and saw a blue light, like the kind that came from computer screens, coming from the last room. I ran to the room and looked in. There, slumped over the desk with his head on the keyboard, was Russell.

Chapter Twelve

Sam came to the room soon after I did.

"Russell? You okay, man?" Sam asked, approaching him.

I followed close behind Sam, and we inched toward Russell while repeating his name.

Sam reached out and put his hand on Russell's back. "Russell?" Sam shook him a little, and Russell's left hand, which had been lying on the keyboard, fell limply to his side.

Sam and I both jumped back. Sam let out a small gasp. I unknowingly held my breath until I started to feel faint. After a moment, Sam reached down to check for a pulse on Russell's neck. His hand stayed still for a few seconds, and then Sam put his hand down and stood up straight. He emphasized each of his next words slowly: "He's dead. Russell is dead."

We both took two steps back. We were breathing heavily, and yet it still felt like I couldn't catch my breath. I didn't know if I should feel sad, scared, or guilty, but the mix of all three made me sick. I grabbed the trash can next to the desk and threw up. I hadn't eaten much today, so it took no time to empty the contents of my stomach, but I continued to hold the trash can in fear I wasn't finished.

"What have we done?" I muttered under my breath. "And what do we do?" My voice grew louder with panic. I had experienced loss in my life, but I had never seen a dead body before, and my knees started to feel weak.

"I'm going to call Detective Clarke." Sam's voice was quiet, as if he could barely get the words out.

"I don't know if we can trust him, Sam. Did you know he was fired?"

"If he was fired for not getting the mark, then I think that is a pretty good indication that we can trust him more than just calling down to the police station. Don't you think?"

I looked back over at Russell, whose head was still resting on his keyboard. The mixed emotions came flooding back, and I bent over with my hands holding the trash can again.

"Scott, you going to be okay, achi?"

I held up my hand to let him know I couldn't answer just yet. My stomach was slowly settling, but my head had started to spin. I wanted this to be a bad dream. I closed my eyes tight and then opened them back up with the hopes that everything would have disappeared and I would wake up in my bed. That didn't happen.

"I know this is hard, Scott, but we have to pull ourselves together. We can't just stay here or leave Russell here, and we need to decide on who to call."

Sam had placed his hand on my back. I admired his strength and leadership. I felt like a failure on every level. I couldn't even stop getting sick long enough to process what had happened.

I took a couple more deep breaths, set down the trash can, and straightened up. "If you think Clarke is the best one to call, do it."

Sam nodded, grabbed my shoulder, and pulled me into a hug. The tears started to flow, and crying made me feel better. Sam withdrew from me, grabbed his phone, and put the call on speaker.

"Hello?" Detective Clarke answered on the first ring.

"Hey, it's Sam Stern."

"Sam! I've been worried about you guys. Is Scott with you? I've been trying to get a hold of him. Are you guys okay?"

"Yeah, about that. I don't know how to put this, but one of our friends is dead and—"

"Dead! Who's dead? What happened?"

Sam paused. He looked like he didn't know where to start. He tilted his head back, closed his eyes, and took a deep breath before continuing. "His name is Russell. He was helping us out, and it looks like someone got to him before we could get back here and check on him, and, well, now we are at his house, and we don't know what to do."

"Okay, first off, don't touch anything."

Sam's eyes grew big as his head turned toward the trash can. "Yeah, that might be a problem."

"You guys! Okay, just stay put and send me the address."

I looked at Sam and shook my head while waving my hand back and forth to make sure he didn't tell him where we were.

"Uhhhh, hold please," Sam said into the phone.

"Hold?" Clarke belted out right before Sam put him on mute.

"What?" Sam asked as he turned toward me.

"Don't tell him where we are at. What if he is in on it?"

"If he was in on it, then he would already know where we were," Sam responded.

"Okay, well, I guess that makes sense, but what if he is partly in on it and wasn't the one who actually killed Russell but is still after us?"

Sam closed his eyes and shook his head. I could tell I was frustrating him, but I also didn't want to take any more chances, especially after losing Russell. "Okay, fine," Sam muttered then took the phone back off mute.

"Hello? You still there? Hello?" Clarke sounded nervous and frustrated.

"Uh, yeah, sorry, phone problems. So, umm, I think I'm going to, uh, I mean, I will text you the address as soon as I look at the number. I remember getting here but don't remember the exact address. I think Scott and I are going to leave to make sure the others are okay," Sam said.

"You guys are way over your head, and you need my help. One of you is dead! DEAD!" Detective Clarke could obviously tell we were trying to avoid him. "This isn't just some game that you can just start over if you mess up."

Sam looked straight up at the ceiling. Detective Clarke and I were putting Sam in the middle of an impossible conversation. He took a deep breath, lowered his head, and began to talk again. "Here are the facts. Scott's letter had a clue about Ted in it, and when he got back to his house that night, his teddy bear was ripped in half on his floor. There is someone or lots of someones, I don't know, out there who have betrayed us. Since you read the letter that night, Scott is hesitant to trust you. The truth is, we don't know who to trust, but I want to trust you because we need you, and we just don't know what to do or who to go to."

There was silence on the other end of the phone. Sam looked at me for reassurance that he had said the right thing, and I nodded.

"Wow, guys. That does change things. Look, I had no idea someone had been back in your house. When I put the patrol car there, I didn't get any reports back until they told me you were pretty much MIA. I heard on the police scanner that you were wanted for questioning regarding a minor infraction on the bus. I thought that was a strange reason to look for someone, and I happened to be parked nearby and saw you running. I followed you to a neighborhood, but when I knocked on the door of the house you went into, nobody was there. I want to help you guys as much as I can, but I don't work on the force anymore. I still have a few friends there, and I will help you out as much as I can. I get that you don't trust me just yet. That's fine. Just text me the address after you guys get out of there. And I will head over there before I call it in."

Sam turned to me, and I nodded.

"Okay. We will text you as soon as we leave," Sam said before he hung up the phone.

I grabbed the trash can to dispose of it on the way back to my house. Before I left, I stared at Russell for a moment. I hated leaving him there. I felt like a horrible person. It was good that Sam was with me to keep us focused on the task at hand so we could make sure this didn't happen to anyone else.

Now, we had the awful job of telling everyone what had happened. Sam called his parents on the way back to my house.

Joe answered on the second ring. "Hey! You guys almost back with the second load?"

"Hey, Dad. I think we screwed up. Like, big time."

"What happened? Is everyone okay?" From her voice, it sounded like Sam's mom was across the room running toward the phone.

"We gave the stuff to Audrey's friend Russell, and when we got to his house to check on him…" Sam could barely make out the words, "he was dead, Dad."

"You guys need to get out of there." There was panic in Joe's voice I'd never heard before; he always sounded so calm and assured. "Russell? Is that the same Russell who was on the news today? There was a guy named Russell that was in the middle of the protest, and there was a lot of heat over his speech."

"We already left, and yeah, that is the same guy. I called Detective Clarke, and he is planning on heading over there and calling it in. Dad, this is our fault."

"Son, you guys don't know that. He stirred up quite a commotion earlier. This could be related to that somehow. Right now, you guys just need to focus on getting everyone back here safe. I think it is time that we start executing our hideout plans. We will load up the trailer with the supplies you bring over from Scott's and start getting everything else over here. Your brother and I have already started bringing stuff to the hideout from the house."

"Okay, I think we can get by with making one last trip. I'll see if everyone can come stay with us tonight, too. I think that would be best, if you are good with that," Sam replied.

"Absolutely, hamud, be safe," Joe said then hung up the phone.

"He hasn't called me *hamud* in years," Sam said, his voice cracking.

Hearing Joe's voice had been a little reassuring. Joe seemed to have a plan for everything. I had known he had a plan to hide all of us once things started getting crazy after the mark became permanent, but he had never told any of us the location of the hiding spot. I didn't even know if it was in the same state. I doubted he had thought we would be needing to go there so soon. I felt like the trouble I was in was sucking in everyone else around me as well.

"I just don't know what to do, Sam," I said. I took a deep breath and put my head into my hands. "I just don't know what to do."

Chapter Thirteen

The door to my house was open when Sam and I pulled up, and Audrey was standing in the doorway. As soon as she saw us, she ran to the car as if she already knew what news we were about to tell her. I barely had gotten the words out when she cried out, "No!" and wrapped her arms around me and sobbed. I stayed outside with her for a few minutes and let her cry. I didn't say anything. I didn't have the words. Sam went inside to tell Carl and Max.

We slowly made our way back into the house, and Carl, Sam, and Max were quietly standing near the door.

"All we can do now is share the video ourselves any way we can to try to get the word out there to warn people," I said, the words coming out slow and soft. The lump in my throat made it hard for me to speak.

"No way am I going to share that video! Absolutely no way!" Max cried out.

I was taken aback by Max's statement. I knew that Max didn't share the same beliefs as the rest of us, but I had still thought he would think it was important to share the information we had found about my dad's company and the mark.

"I mean, he isn't wrong, not wanting to share it," Carl stepped in on Max's behalf. "Sharing the video on our own page could get us all put on a watch list, or even worse, end up like Russell."

"I get what you are all saying," Sam started, "but whoever killed Russell was fast. Someone went in and out of there *before* Russell could send that video. That means it wasn't just some government watch group. Whoever did it wanted to prevent it from going out, not punish him for sending it. We also forgot to mention that we saw the car that chased us tonight leaving Russell's house right before we got there. I don't think that's a coincidence. If that's the case, then we are probably all safer if we just send it now. Whoever tried to stop Russell will come after us next if they think we are still going to try to get the video out there, but if we share it now, then it's too late. Sending it could, in fact, save our lives."

I agreed with Sam. Sending the video was the only way I could save my friends. I ran up the stairs to my bedroom, and everyone followed me. I sat at my desk while the others were still climbing up the stairs. All I needed to do was log in to my email and share the video. It seemed simple.

My mouth filled up with water, and I had difficulty swallowing. I pushed the power button on my laptop, and…nothing happened. I checked the power cables. Everything looked like it was plugged in and ready to go. By the time everyone had arrived at my room, I had unplugged it and was plugging it back in, but still, nothing happened.

"Ugh! You've got to be kidding me. My computer worked just fine the last time I was here. Now nothing. Someone had to have tampered with it."

"Just use your phone," Carl suggested.

I gave him the look that Mila usually gave to Sam and Nate, eyes darting at him then rolling into the back of my head. "Dude, my phone is still at your house, remember?"

"Done! I sent it." Sam stood in the doorway holding his phone.

"You sent what? The video?" Max's sounded both scared and angry.

"Sam!" I shouted. "I wanted to be the one to—"

"I know, but it would have been because I talked you into it. I know what I did, and I don't have any regrets," Sam interrupted me.

Within seconds, Carl had his phone out and had sent the video as well. "Done and done!" he said proudly.

Max threw up his hands then placed them on top of his head as he paced my bedroom.

"If it reaches just one person, it will be worth it to me, too," Audrey said, as she whipped out her phone and shared the video.

"I gotta get out of here!" Max sounded like he was having a nervous breakdown. He was still pacing around the room, and his breathing was getting deeper and faster.

"Max! Calm down. If we stick together, we will be better off. There is safety in numbers. Max…Max?" I tried to get him to stop pacing, to just stop for a moment and listen to me.

He was mumbling something about getting killed, failing, and how he was too young to die before he said, more clearly, "I gotta go." He left my room and ran down the stairs, and we all followed him. He opened the front door and kept walking without shutting the door behind him or looking to see if anyone was coming with him.

"Max! Where are you going?" I called out after him.

"Home, I gotta go," Max yelled back without turning.

We all stood on the driveway and watched as Max took off down the street toward his house. Just when he had driven out of view, we saw headlights approaching from the opposite direction.

I no longer felt the need to run from anyone. I had found everything I had needed to find, and we had sent out the information, so I remained where I was as the car approached. Before it pulled up next to us, I could tell by the headlights that it was a different car than the one we had seen leave Russell's house. The car came to a slow stop, and the engine shut off. The driver's door opened, and out came Detective Clarke.

"I figured I could find you here. Didn't think you'd all be standing outside just waiting for me." Clarke looked like he always did. He had on his shirt and tie even though he was no longer a detective, and his shirt had a brown stain on it, probably from eating lunch in his car. He still had a bit of a sandwich in one hand.

None of us responded. I didn't know whether to ask if he had taken care of Russell, why he was here, or if I was in trouble somehow, so I waited for him to talk first.

"Anyways," Clarke continued, throwing the last bite of his sandwich into the yard. "I called one of my friends that still works for the department. Told him I got a tip then told him I would pass the tip along since I no longer work there but I could stay at the house till he arrived in case I saw something."

He waited a few seconds for us to respond, but none of us said a thing.

"Anyway, your friend is definitely gone. Thing about it is, in all appearances, it looks like a heart attack. My guess is they would rule it as a natural cause of death except for the way I called it in…with a tip."

Sam and I looked at each other, then at Carl and Audrey, then at each other again, then back at Clarke. I was still unsure what to say, so I kept quiet, and Clarke kept talking.

"I guess my question is, are you sure your friend was murdered? Code 36-12-1 should give us access to the autopsy reports. The problem is with the whole tip thing. They may consider it a pending criminal investigation and withhold the reports from the public."

"I think that you should look at the video that he was trying to get out and then ask us again if we think he was murdered," Sam replied. "I'll text you the link."

"Okay, let's check it out," Clarke said. He pulled out his phone and clicked the link Sam had sent him. For the next few minutes, the only thing that could be heard was my disguised voice from the video. The longer Clarke watched, the wider his eyes got. "This is exactly the information and evidence that I've been searching for. Where did you find all this?"

"The letter from Scott's mom we read with you at the station led us to it," Carl explained.

"Scott, you sure you want this to be posted?" Clarke asked me. "This incriminates your dad's company big time."

"My mom led me here for a reason, and I don't think it was to help cover it all up. This is unquestionably something I needed to do," I replied.

"I think you all should find a safer place to stay." Clarke seemed genuinely worried.

"We have a plan," I reassured him.

Clarke nodded. I still was unsure how much I could trust him, but he didn't ask what our plan was as I'd expected him to. He looked like he was deep in thought, working out his next move.

"I may need to leave town for a couple of days. If you guys need me for anything at all, just text me. I should be able to be back in less than two hours," Clarke said, then he ducked into his car and drove off without further explanation.

"I think you should all come back to my house and stay there for the night. It's not that I think anything will happen now that the video is out, but if I could give this week one word to describe it, it would be *unpredictable,* for sure. I think, at the very least, there is safety in numbers," Sam said as we all watched Detective Clarke's taillights fade in the distance.

"As long as your parents are both okay with it, I would feel much better staying with you all," Audrey replied.

"Should we go get Max?" I asked the group. "I want to make sure he is okay. I kind of don't want to let any of you out of my sight at this point."

"I mean, I get that and all, but maybe he just needs some time. He seemed pretty freaked out, and he may feel safer at home. No one at his house shared that video, but we all did, ya know?" Audrey sounded like a voice of reason though I still didn't like the idea of splitting up.

"Okay, yeah, I get it," I replied.

We loaded up the rest of the supplies I thought we might need. I ran upstairs to grab my last duffle bag along with my Bible. I started to rush down the stairs but stopped and looked back at my parents' room. I walked back and into their room and looked at the room just the way my parents had left it. I opened their closet. All my parents' clothes were still there, untouched.

I grabbed one of my dad's sweaters and held it up to my face. I could imagine his smell. I started flipping through more clothes and realized I was now the same size as my dad. I grabbed a couple of his shirts and threw them in my bag. I grabbed his Indianapolis Colts jersey and put it on. It fit perfectly. He used to take my mom to the games. I'd even gotten to go to a game with him once. I'd worn this exact jersey to the game, and at the time, I'd swam in it.

I walked to the nightstand and picked up the framed picture of the three of us standing in front of a gray backdrop. There had been a family picture day at our church, and my mom had insisted we all dress up and get our pictures taken. I had been eight and hated having to wear a tie, but in the picture, we all looked genuinely happy. I smiled and dropped the picture into my duffle bag before heading back down the stairs.

"Sweet jersey," Carl said.

"Thanks, it was my dad's, and now it seems to fit me. Guess I'm built like him."

We all piled back into the car and then stopped at Carl's house to pick up some of his clothes and personal items. I grabbed my phone, and then we headed to Audrey's house. Carl seemed a little tense on the ride.

"What's up, man?" I asked him.

"I don't know, I just have a bad feeling. I texted my aunt since she wasn't home just to tell her where I was and where I was going, but she hasn't answered yet. Then it dawned on me that I hadn't heard from her all day. So I checked my phone, and I hadn't heard from her at all yesterday either. She is usually the one checking up on me, so it never dawned on me that I should be checking up on her. Now I'm kind of worried about her." Carl's voice had a slight quiver to it that made me believe he was choking back tears.

"Sorry, Carl, maybe it's just something as silly as her phone battery dying or something like that. When she gets home, she will get the note you left her and text you back, I'm sure of it. She knows you've been hanging out with me now that school is out and there isn't anywhere that you have needed to be, so she is probably just giving you a little taste of adult freedom. I'm sure she's fine." I kept talking, listing all the reasons I thought Carl's aunt was fine, for my own sake as much as for Carl's.

We all stayed in the car while Audrey ran into her house to grab her stuff. She couldn't have been in there longer than five minutes before she came back out, and we headed back to Sam's for the night.

I lay on the couch with Bucket for at least two hours without the relief of sleep. Russell had seemed like a great guy. We had only just talked to him about God, and he had seemed curious about Christianity and how it related to everything going on around the world. I wished I had talked to him more about it.

The fan on the ceiling made a faint ticking noise as it spun above the room. I stopped focusing on my insecurities and focused on the constant ticking of the fan. I started to pray, but I kept stopping. I didn't know what to pray for. I didn't know what to do with everything that had been happening, and I didn't know what to say to God. As I tried to focus on the words to say, I fell asleep.

Chapter Fourteen

The next thing I knew, Mila was patting my shoulder. "I hate to have to wake you two up since you seem to be sleeping so soundly and snuggly, but it's Sunday morning, and we have people coming over to have church."

Bucket jumped down and out of my arms as if he had understood Mila.

Sunday? Church? I hadn't paid attention to the time or day all week and felt an odd sense of normalcy.

"How many people usually come over?" I asked. This was probably the first time in my life that I was looking forward to church even though it was a lot different than it used to be.

"Well, let's see. It started out with just us for a while. Then our next-door neighbors started coming. They met Audrey while getting their car worked on one day, and she came. Then a couple of people from around town that knew Joe came. Last week, we had eight people over, not including the family. We also have been connecting online with other groups that have been meeting at different homes."

It made me happy to know that there were other people in the world that had the same beliefs and wanted the same things.

"Oh, I forgot to mention. A couple of the people who come over to have church with us saw your video last night. Some have neighbors who were debating getting the mark, so they reached out to those neighbors to share the video. Isn't that great? I'm so excited it's reaching people."

I thought it was very odd since we had only just posted the video late the night before. "Really? What time did they call your neighbors?"

"Oh, I don't know exactly what time it was. I do know I was cleaning up after dinner, and we ate around six, so I would say a little after seven last night," Mila responded.

None of my friends had shared the video until after nine last night at the earliest. Maybe Mila had her times wrong. Regardless, I was glad it seemed to be making an impact already. I checked my phone for any missed messages and calls—it had been charging overnight, so I hadn't checked it since I had retrieved it last night—and then I called Max to see if he wanted to come to the Bible study.

Max's phone rang several times, but there was no answer. I wanted to assume he just wasn't awake yet though I still felt a twinge of worry since he wasn't with us. After spending a few minutes deleting messages, I tried again, but there was still no answer.

A few people arrived at the door, and Joe and Mila greeted them and escorted them to where I was sitting. Joe wore his kippah. He said he did it as a sign of reverence and respect but it wasn't something that was required. Bucket stayed on the floor in front of me. Mila had already cleaned up our sheets, and Audrey and Sam followed in behind the visitors. I had never been one for socializing with people I didn't know, so I just smiled and nodded my head at each person that came in and sat down. I felt awkward but still wanted to make an effort of some sort, but the moment anyone made eye contact with me, I averted my eyes to anywhere else in the room.

Joe seemed like such a natural while talking to people he had never met before. He would walk right up to them with his hand outstretched, and before long, they would be laughing and talking as if they had known each other forever.

When we were all sitting down, Mila passed around a piece of paper with sheet music for the song, "Turn Your Eyes Upon Jesus." Mila sat down, and we all started to sing. I recognized the song as soon as we started singing. I was sure I had sung it dozens of times in church with my mom, but I had never taken the words to heart until today.

After the song, Joe prayed and then began talking about a man named Jehoshaphat. I thought I had known a lot of Bible stories, but I didn't know anything about this man at all. He was a king. I thought kings should have all the answers and do things without fear, but King Jehoshaphat was scared and said, "We do not know what to do, but our eyes are on You."

I couldn't recall how many times that week I had said, "I don't know what to do." Here was a king, the ruler of Judah, and he, too, didn't know what to do, but he had prayed to God and even had singers go out singing praises and thanking God for His faithfulness before God did anything. I knew I needed to take a lesson from this king. Instead of always focusing on not knowing what to do next, I needed to look to God and praise and thank Him for all He has done. He helped me find the letter, was with us when we were being chased, protected us, and guided our paths the entire time.

Joe stood up from his seat. "I would like to invite you all to step outside for a moment. There are four people here today that have accepted Jesus as their Lord and Savior and have asked to demonstrate their obedience to God through Baptism."

Everyone followed Joe outside where, one by one, four of us stepped up to the water trough Joe had set up earlier. Joe baptized two of the church newcomers alongside Carl and me in the name of the Father, the Son, and the Holy Spirit. Carl threw up his hands and rejoiced when he came up out of the water. I had never been so sure of any decision I had ever made in my life. I was the last one to step out of the trough, and I grabbed Carl and hugged him like never before.

Everyone standing around us began to shuffle back inside the house. Joe had pulled some of the new people off to the side to talk to them more about Christ and how he came to believe He was the Messiah. The rest of the us went to the kitchen to grab some of the food that Mila had put out. After I changed my clothes, I waited in the front room of the house to give people space in the kitchen. I was staring out the front window waiting for the others to make their way into the dining room when I noticed a man standing across the street, leaning up against a car, and looking at the house.

Sam walked into the front room with a plate, snacking on some veggies and dip.

"You know this guy?" I asked, nodding toward the man standing across the street.

"No, I've never seen that car before, either," Sam replied. "Has he been staring at the house long?"

"As long as I've been standing here, he has," I said.

"Is that the same man that has been following you?" Sam asked.

"Nah, definitely not the same guy."

The man was extremely slender. His face looked rough, and even from across the street, I could tell he hadn't shaved in a while, though he didn't have a full beard. His hair was dark and cut short, and his clothes looked well-worn. In the past, I probably would have been nervous about his presence, but I felt more curious this time.

"What are we all looking at?" Carl asked as he popped a chip in his mouth.

"There is a guy standing outside just staring at the house," I replied. "I think I'm going to go talk to him. Maybe he heard about the Bible study but didn't want to just come in. I'll let him know that it's over but he can still come in and eat something and we can talk to him."

Sam patted me on the back. "Proud of you, man, I know it's not easy for you to break out of your shell, but just in case, I'll keep an eye on you from the window."

I turned to Sam and laughed. "Thanks, man. Come on, Bucket."

Bucket jumped up from his seat, and we walked out the front door. The man didn't react as he saw me walking out of the house toward him. I told myself to be nice, smile, and offer my hand just like Joe would have.

"Hello!" I said with my hand outstretched when I arrived in front of the man, who was still leaning on the car. "I'm—"

"Scott, Scott Killian. I know who you are," he said.

I was taken aback. I had been prepared to invite this man in and had to readjust my train of thought, but all I managed to get out was, "Huh?"

He reached into his pocket and pulled out what looked like a tin of mints that he opened to reveal a row of cigarettes. He pulled out a cigarette and stuck the end of it into his mouth then offered the can to me.

"Uh, no, thanks, I don't smoke," I said, still completely confused.

"Yeah, probably for the best. I've been rolling my own now for, uh, well, since I was about nineteen, I guess. They are hard to come by these days. Figured I'd quit, but now that I know the world is pretty much coming to an end, thanks to you, that is, I figured I would just keep on smoking, I guess."

"Thanks to me? What do you—?"

He put up his hand. "Listen, kid," he started. Hearing him call me *kid* made me think of Russell, though he was much older, and I felt a sinking feeling in the pit of my stomach. "Russell sent the video to me. I'm the one that got it online."

I wasn't sure what to say. I didn't know if he knew what had happened to Russell. "Look, about Russell—"

"I know about Russell. I think Russell knew his time was going to be short. He put himself out there way too much if you ask me. I prefer to be in the background myself. Then there's you: Scott Killian, age eighteen, likes playing video games and drinking Coke, son of the man who helped launch this huge mess and now trying to bring down his daddy's legacy."

"How did you—?"

He held up his hand again. "I looked into you. I needed to find out if I could trust you. What I can't figure out is why hide who you are in the video? Once this video gets out, your dad will figure out it came from you, right? I mean, there is no way you guys are tight, right?"

"My mom and dad both disappeared a few years ago." I figured now that I was out of high school and eighteen, there was no need to keep hiding their disappearances.

"Hmm, well, that is very interesting, indeed." He took another long puff on his cigarette and blew it out of the right side of his mouth.

"Why interesting?" I asked.

"Well, I do my homework, and I am usually pretty good at figuring out that kind of stuff. I looked at the bank records, and there has been money moving in his account," he said.

"I never reported them missing, so I kept all the autopay stuff the same. Plus, I used their card for groceries and stuff that I needed," I explained.

"I see, huh, yeah, still interesting." He squinted at me through the smoke billowing around his head.

"And why is that?" I asked.

"Uh, well, let me ask you, did you get the mark?"

"No. Of course, not. It would be dumb to make a video warning people against it and then go and get it myself."

"Yeah, didn't think so. I think the money must be getting moved around by someone else who has access to the accounts that also has the chip. But to be honest, I wasn't looking for that, so now I will have to dig some more. Hmm. Well, kid, I gotta scram."

"Wait, what do you mean someone else has access to it?"

"Well, after the chip became mandatory to use, there was money still being transferred in and out of that account. At least, that is what it looked like at the time. Maybe I'm wrong. See ya around, kid."

"Wait, what's your name?" I asked.

"Well, you see, kid, that is more on a need-to-know basis. For now, you can call me O-one."

"Owen? So that's not your real name?" I asked.

"It's more like the numbers zero and one, like binary code. So, not my real name, but, yeah, just call me Owen. That is what all my friends call me these days," he said as he chuckled and blew out another puff of smoke.

"Wait, so that's it? You just came by to tell me you know me, check to see if I have the mark, and then take off?" I asked.

"I needed to find out if I could trust you. It just wouldn't make sense that you would want to bring down your daddy's company if you were working for them, but you can never be too careful, so I wanted to see for myself if you had the mark. It does raise some other questions, though. I need to look at some things. If I need you, I'll find you." He threw his cigarette onto the ground and opened his car door.

"What other questions does it raise?" I asked.

"Be careful who you trust, kid." With that, he slammed his car door shut and started the engine. He rolled forward a little before rolling down his window and asking, "Did your dad's company know that your parents disappeared?"

"I never told anyone. One person called me from the company a few years ago and asked about my dad, but I told him my dad was traveling for business, and I haven't heard from anyone since."

Owen nodded. "Good to know," he said, then he took off.

As I watched his car, which looked like a very old Mustang that'd had some serious modifications done to it, pull away, I saw the license plate flip over and change to a new plate number. I looked back toward the house and could see Sam and Carl in the window watching me.

Sam threw up his arms as if to ask, *What happened?* I threw up my hands and smiled to say, *I have no idea.*

Chapter Fifteen

Bucket and I walked back into the house as people started to leave. I nodded and smiled politely as they passed me in the doorway, still not managing to speak to any of them. I headed back to the family room and grabbed my duffle bag to pack my toothbrush and deodorant, and I pulled out my family picture. Audrey saw it and sat next to me on the couch.

"I remember it was on a Friday," I started. "My mom had just started dinner, and my dad wasn't home from work yet. My mom asked me to take out the trash, and I ran upstairs to my room and pretended I didn't hear her. I started playing a video game, just this stupid warrior golf game. I realized I had never heard my dad come home, and I was getting hungry. I went downstairs, and dinner was sitting in a pot on the counter. It wasn't warm at all. I called out for my mom several times but didn't hear anything. I heard sirens in the background and realized they had been going off for a while. When I looked outside, I saw my mom's car still sitting in the driveway. I went back inside and sat at the dinner table and just waited. With every passing minute, I felt more and more scared.

"I got up and took the trash out. That is when I noticed that my dad's car was still not back. I ran back inside and ran upstairs and looked in the bedroom. I thought maybe my mom had gotten tired of waiting, too, so she had lain down and fallen asleep or something, but I never saw either one of them again. I blamed myself for never listening to them. Every day for the first week afterward, I would come home and expect to find them there. I thought they would just show back up as if nothing had happened. I remember crying myself to sleep a few times. It took a while before I even admitted to Carl or Sam that they were gone. I don't think I admitted it to myself right away, you know?"

Audrey put her hand on my back. "I'm sorry you went through that. At least now you know you will see them again."

"Thanks, I know. I hope that in the meantime I can make the best of the time we are here. I want to head over to Max's house to see if he is okay. He hasn't answered his phone, and I think we kind of freaked him out last night."

Sam came in and stood behind Audrey. "I think that's a good idea. I'll get the keys."

"I want to come, too," Audrey said.

I bent down to pet Bucket. "You'll have to stay here with Mila again. We may not have room for you in the car if we find Max, but I'll be back."

As we headed toward the door, we passed Carl in the kitchen filling his plate up for the fourth time. "Let me grab one more of these fire meatballs for my plate, and I'll meet you guys out there."

At the car, Audrey and I slid into the backseat and Carl jumped into the front, barely able to balance everything on his plate. I noticed a meatball lying on the sidewalk between the car and the house and shook my head and smiled.

"What's funny?" Audrey questioned.

"'And then my poor meatball, it rolled out the door,'" I said, laughing. "It was a song my grandpa used to sing to me." I pointed at the lonely meatball on the sidewalk.

"Oh, man! That was my last meatball, too!" Carl said with his mouth full. "Such a waste."

"We aren't going back for the meatball, so buckle up," Sam said.

The ride over to Max's house was nice. It was sunny and calm outside with no sign of earthquakes. I was beginning to feel that we were finally done being followed. I told the others about Owen and that he was able to get the video out there for the world to see.

"So we did it! It's all over!" Carl exclaimed.

"I hate to burst your bubble, but just because we were able to get this accomplished doesn't mean that everything is going to be rainbows and butterflies the next few years. In fact, we need to prepare ourselves for the worst, which is still to come," Sam said somberly as we pulled into Max's driveway.

"Just let me have my five minutes of peace, joy, and meatballs with nachos," Carl said. He threw his last nacho into his mouth before opening his car door. "I'll walk you to the door, sir."

"Why, thank you," I replied as I exited the car. We walked up to the door of the small blue house. The paint was chipped, and the beams on the porch looked rotted. I rang the doorbell, and we waited for a moment before the door opened. Max's mom stood in the doorway.

"Good morning, Scott. Good morning, Carl. How are you boys doing? Been a while." Max's mom was at least ten years older than my mom. She was always very sweet, but I had not spoken to her much. We hardly ever hung out at Max's house, and when we did stop by, we rarely saw his parents.

"Yeah, we're good. How are you, Mrs. Lambert?" I asked.

"I'm doing just fine. What can I do for you boys?" she asked.

"We were hoping Max could hang out, is all," I replied.

"Oh, I figured you knew he was working today," she said.

"I thought the shop was closed on Sundays," Carl said.

"Oh, it is. He isn't at the shop today, he is at his other part-time job," she insisted.

Carl and I looked at each other in confusion. "Since when did Max have another part-time job?"

Max's mother looked equally confused by the question. "It's his personal assistant job to that one gentleman. Oh, I can't remember his name. Surely, he has told you about it. He's been working for him for a few years now, ever since he has been able to work, I believe."

I had never heard of Max having any other job other than at the shop, but I didn't want to concern his mom, so I said, "Oh, okay, yeah, I must have forgotten or something. Just tell him we stopped by when you see him. Sorry to bother you, Mrs. L."

I turned and headed back to the car. Carl quickly caught up with me.

"What the heck does she mean about another job that he has had for years?" Carl asked.

"Is Max doing better than he was last night?" Sam asked when we entered the car.

"I guess you could say that," I replied. "He isn't home because he is apparently at his other part-time job that he has had for the last few years."

Sam turned around in his seat with the same look on his face that Carl and I both had at the door. "Wait, what?"

"It seemed odd at first, but then I thought maybe he hasn't been lying to us. Maybe he has been lying to his mom. He spends a lot of time with us, and maybe his mom wanted him home more, so he made up a story about having another part-time job. Makes sense to me now that I think about it. If he isn't working, he is usually with us, so that has to be it." I was trying to convince myself more than I was trying to convince the rest of them.

"I don't know, it seems like he hides things from you guys a lot," Audrey said.

"What do you mean, he hides stuff from us?" I asked. "I have never caught Max in a lie or even had a notion he was hiding anything from me or anyone else. He has never even asked me to keep a secret from Carl or Sam before."

"You never found it odd that he was still working at the shop the day that I left when I chose to lose my job over getting the mark?" Audrey asked.

My stomach sank, and I felt a tightness in my chest. It had never dawned on me that Max could have gotten the mark. We had talked about it in the past, and he had never seemed opposed to it, but I figured he would wait.

Memories flooded my mind: the ads on the bus playing when he sat next to me were the same ads that targeted people with the mark; he had been offered a promotion at work just days before Audrey had lost her job for not taking the mark; he had ridden the bus to work without any problem the same day that I had gotten Gary in trouble for riding it without the mark.

"Do you guys for real think Max went ahead and got the mark? And if so, what does that even have to do with him having another job that he never told us about?"

"Well, I'm guessing it shows us there is a lot more to Max than any of us realize," Sam said.

"Wait, hold up. This is Max we are talking about. He wouldn't just go and get the mark, and he wouldn't hide anything from us. I mean, it's not like we would hold it against him for having another job, especially if he has had it as long as we have known him. He also never acted secretive about the mark. He even said he was considering it, so why bother hiding it if he was open about it in the past? None of this is adding up." I was upset, but I also knew that logically speaking, Max was hiding something from us one way or another.

"So where should we go next then?" Sam asked. "Remember I need to be back with the car by this afternoon. I promised my dad I would help them load up supplies and bring them over to our hideaway shelter."

"Speaking of loading up supplies, I think we need to circle back to the storage unit at some point. There were a lot of files there, and I'm sure there is a ton of stuff we missed. We could also grab some of the supplies from the unit and take them to your parents' house. For now, why don't we just swing by the shop to make sure that Max isn't there?" I said.

When we arrived at the shop, Sam and Carl stayed in the car while Audrey and I stepped out to look around. The doors were all closed and locked. The lights were all off, and there didn't seem to be any movement inside when we looked in the windows.

"I don't think he's here," Audrey said.

"Yeah, I know. It was a shot in the dark, but for my own piece of mind I had to look."

"I get it," Audrey replied.

Audrey and I were heading back to the car when she placed her hand on my shoulder. Her hand felt warm and inviting. I couldn't help but think about how crazy it was that I could like someone so much after only knowing them for such a short time.

As we made our way back to the front of the building, I noticed an old black Mustang parked just a few car lengths' away from Sam's car.

"Hey, I think that's Owen's car," I said to Audrey. "I'm going to go say hi. He just may be the guy who can help us."

Before I could approach the car, Owen stepped out and placed a cigarette in his mouth. He walked to the front of his car and leaned on the hood.

"Hey, Owen, how did you know I was going to be here?" I asked.

"You're very presumptuous, kid. Meeting you here is just a mere coincidence. However, I did see you snooping around that building over there, so you're not very inconspicuous," Owen replied.

"Ha, yeah, I guess I need to work on my detective skills. Speaking of, since you are here, can I ask a small favor?" I asked.

"As long as you know that favors are usually returned," he said with a smirk as smoke trickled out of the corner of his mouth.

I smiled. I was beginning to like Owen a lot. "Absolutely. So I have this friend that I have been close with for the past few years, and he ended up MIA today. I went by his house, and his mom mentioned a part-time job that I didn't know anything about, and—"

"And you want to know what this job is and what kind of secrets he's been keeping from you, huh?" Owen interrupted.

"Well, I guess I was wanting to know what happened to him," I replied.

"Look, kid, it's okay to question your friend when you find out your friend has been hiding something from you. You're not wrong to be curious. If it turns out to be nothing, you can ask him why he would keep something so trivial from you. I get that you are still concerned about him, but you have other friends to be concerned about as well," Owen said.

"Yeah, I guess you're right. Thing is, it seems like he got the mark as well, and I didn't know about that, either. Anyway, this is one of the places he works, so we decided to check it out just to see if he was here."

"Got it. What's his name?" Owen asked.

"Max, Max Lambert. Uh, you need his address or anything?"

"That is remarkably interesting. Nah, I'm sure I can figure it out as long as that isn't just an alias."

Owen's words hit me hard. "An alias? No way. I've known him for years. He was still in school when we met."

Owen blew another puff of smoke out of the corner of his mouth, smirked again, and said, "Yeah, we'll see, though as of right now, I have a good hunch it's his real name."

"Do you want my phone number?" I asked.

"Probably best to keep our conversations in person and not over the phone," Owen replied. "And I wanted to tell you something else."

"Oh, yeah?" I asked, noticing at the same time Audrey standing awkwardly about fifteen feet back. I gave her a quick smile to reassure her that I was good.

"Just like I thought, someone has indeed gotten into your bank account."

My attention snapped from Audrey back to Owen. "What? Who?"

"I'm not entirely sure. They haven't just been moving money out of the account but back into it as well. To me, that is more suspicious than just hacking into someone's account and stealing their money. A chunk of the money was pulled out and transferred into another account recently, after the chip mandate."

"Who's account?"

"Funny you should ask," Owen said. "The name on the account was Max Lambert."

None of this made sense. "Please tell me you're joking."

"Afraid not," Owen said.

"Well, how?"

"That I hadn't figured out just yet. I wasn't quite sure who this Max guy was. I came up here just to see if there was anything I could get off him since he also had money going into his account from this place, but now that I know it's your missing friend, I will be sure to look more into it from a different angle. Since he had another job you didn't know about, I think I'll start there, but the only other money he was getting was from your account. You going to be home later today?"

"Actually, I think we are going to go back to Sam's house for a while," I replied.

"If I find anything, I'll come by," Owen said as he let out his last puff of smoke. He threw his cigarette onto the ground and stepped on it with the front of his shoe.

I returned to Audrey and grabbed her hand, and we headed back to the car without saying a word to each other. I had never held her hand before, but I needed the reassurance, and she seemed not to mind.

In the car, I held her hand again. I was hesitant to tell everyone what Owen had told me. I didn't know Owen, and it was possible he could have been lying to me, though I didn't think he was. Mostly, I felt if I told my friends what Owen had said, then I would somehow be betraying Max and giving up on him.

On the other hand, I didn't want to betray my friends by keeping this information from them.

"There is no easy way to say this. Owen said he had looked into my accounts because it looked like there was some fishy stuff going on when I met up with him at Sam's last time. He said a chunk of the money had been transferred out of my parents' account and into another account. When I asked the name on the account, he said the name was…Max Lambert."

Chapter Sixteen

As Sam drove us back to his parents' house, everyone in the car was confused and upset.

"I think we should take this information as potentially true but not dismiss Max just yet either," Sam said. "I think it just means we need to be cautious if and when he resurfaces, but we need to still try and see if we can find him and if he is okay. Even if the money was put into his name, we don't know how it got there. I honestly don't think that Max could do this on his own, and it might not necessarily be his idea. We just don't know enough to jump to any conclusions either way."

"I agree," I said. "We need to be careful, but we need to treat this as if Max could be in trouble, as right now, he is missing."

"Dude, this is just crazy." Carl had been shaking his head in disbelief since I'd shared Owen's findings. "Like, for real. One of us is missing. *Missing!* That Russell dude died. We've been chased by a car. And to think I wanted to go into law enforcement and deal with this kind of stuff all the time. My guidance counselor needs to be fired."

I couldn't help but chuckle. The more I thought about Carl dealing with any kind of police work on a daily basis, the more I laughed. I guessed my nervous laughter, which had turned uncontrollable, was a coping mechanism. "Yeah, I think you're right there, Carl, your guidance counselor should consider finding a different job!"

Sam and Audrey joined me in chuckling.

"Nope, just no. This is not for me." Carl stopped shaking his head long enough to look back at me. "Read my lips. Fired, Miss Wallman needs to be fired." He turned back around and continued shaking his head.

We pulled into Sam's driveway, and before I let go of Audrey's hand, she pulled me close to her and gave me a big hug.

"I wish I could tell you everything is going to be okay, but we know things are going to be hard. I can tell you that God is with you through all of this, and I am here for you, too," Audrey said before gently kissing me on the cheek.

Her reassurance was appreciated, and I wanted to tell her so, but all I could do was nod and smile. The kiss on the cheek made me feel like butterflies were in my stomach, and I was at a loss for words.

Mila opened the front door as we were getting out of the car, and Inspector Bucket ran toward me and jumped on me, licking my face and wagging his tail. I was glad he had missed me as much as I had missed him. Joe had parked a trailer at the back of the house into which they were loading supplies, clothes, and food. Sam grabbed his mom and brought her around back to where Joe was to tell them about Max and Owen.

Afterward, Joe came into the house to find me. "I know you guys have all been through a lot in such a short period of time. Just know we consider you boys family. Our next step is getting a place ready that we can all go to that will be safe. Not just for us but for our other brothers and sisters in Christ as well. I know it hasn't been that long since you and Carl both accepted Christ. I am amazed at how much God has used you in just a short time. If you ever need anything, we are family now."

Joe's actions had always been enough to let us know he cared for us and would do anything for us, but I appreciated his words all the same. "Thank you, Joe. Since we are talking about the next steps and all, I was thinking, maybe we could go down to the storage unit and bring some stuff back here. There were a lot of supplies and food, but I also wanted to go back through the files. We were in a hurry last time we went, and I would like to see if there is anything we missed."

"That is a promising idea. I wish I could go down with you guys myself, but I have some people meeting me here on and off all day bringing supplies and helping us transfer stuff to the shelter. I am curious about those files, though. Mila is cooking us up some lunch now. You guys should head down there after you eat. You should also pack food in case you get stuck down there for dinner. Knowing you guys, I'm sure this will be an adventure."

We all piled into the dining room, and Joe said the blessing. Mila had hamburgers with all the fixings already on the table. Carl made himself a double cheeseburger that he couldn't fit into his mouth, so he ended up taking it apart and putting half of it back together.

Mila kept looking at Audrey and me and smiling, which made me blush. When Joe noticed Mila's stares, he said, "Well, I think this is the first time one of you had a girlfriend at the dining room table."

Mila smacked his arm with her napkin. "Joe!"

"What? What did I say?" Joe asked as if he were innocent, but we all knew him too well. He laughed. "My apologies, Audrey, but these yahoos know that I like to rustle their feathers and give them a hard time. I'm sure you think Scott is very cute and charming."

"Joe!" Mila yelled, swooshing her napkin at him again.

"What? I thought I was being nice," Joe said as Audrey's face turned a shade of red so deep it almost matched the streaks in her hair.

"Yosef Stern, you can be so uncouth sometimes," Mila said.

We all chuckled, even Audrey. I liked Audrey a lot, but I had never had a girlfriend before. I didn't know if she was my girlfriend now or if it was something we both had to acknowledge in a conversation, but I was too embarrassed to bring it up to her.

I was halfway through my burger when I looked out the window and saw a Mustang pull up across the street. I wiped my mouth with my napkin and stood up. "Excuse me, I will be right back."

Owen was waiting for me outside of his car when I walked outside. I was both anxious and excited to talk to him. I wanted to find out more about Max, and yet, at the same time, I didn't.

I nodded at Owen, and he returned the nod.

"Listen, kid, I still don't have all the answers for you. The fact is, what I found may lead to more questions than answers. I didn't find any proof that he had any job secret or otherwise other than the car shop."

"Well, that's good, isn't it?" I asked.

"On the surface, it would seem so, but I decided to pull up bank transactions again and went further back. He has been transferring money to himself from your account for about three years now," Owen said.

"So you think he got my bank information from my house and started stealing from me here and there since we became friends?" I asked.

"Maybe, but I think it would be more complicated than just that. Plus, he was only taking out small amounts at a time. It was like a couple hundred dollars every so often, but then the last transaction was closer to almost ten grand all at once."

"I had ten thousand dollars left in that account?" I about choked on my spit.

"Oddly enough, there was still money being put into the account. There was more money in the account when that ten thousand dollars got transferred to Max than before Max first started stealing from it," Owen said. "It also looks like most of the ten K was transferred back out of Max's account into another blockchain with Max's name on it and then scattered across several other accounts, and I lost the trail on it. Money is still being transferred into your parents' account through your dad's company quite often, too."

I shook my head and placed my hands on my hips. I looked up at the window and saw Carl turned in his chair staring out at me while eating what appeared to be another burger.

"Listen, kid, I'm going to dig more into this, and don't worry, I'm not considering this another favor. At this point, I'm just as intrigued as you are," Owen continued.

"Thanks for letting me know. We are going to be heading back to the storage unit shortly to look through some more of the files my parents left me about Killian Tech Innovations. Some bad things are tied up in my dad's company."

"If someone there knew your dad went missing and also knew you never reported it, they may be using his account to launder money. They could easily set up his account to accept funds in the form of a salary being directly deposited and then transfer money out to someone like Max from his personal account. This seems like it was done from someone within the company and a bit above Max's capabilities, but I don't know your friend that well."

"Within the company, huh? Have you come across the name Steven Whittaker by any chance?"

"Oddly enough, there was a small deposit transferred into an account with that name on it several years ago after the disappearances. I think it was about a grand. It was a one-time thing but still odd enough that I looked into that as well. He also works at your dad's company."

"Yeah, he is the guy that runs the company when my dad is traveling for business and stuff," I agreed.

"Hardly!" Owen replied. "Not sure what gave you that idea. He is definitely lower-level management. The entire business was never taken out of your dad's name, but the face of the company has been a lady named Genevieve Barts."

My stomach sank, and I grew nauseous. I nodded, not knowing what to say let alone think. "I appreciate you looking for me. If you need to find me, you can leave a message for me here with Joe or Mila. They are good people. You can trust them."

"Alright, kid, good luck. I'm interested to know if you turn up anything new as well," Owen said as he ducked back into his car. "Just be careful out there."

"You too, man." I smacked the roof of the Mustang and headed back to the house. Before I walked in, I tried calling Max again. I wasn't sure what I would say if he answered, but the call went to voicemail, so I hung up and went inside.

Carl and Audrey were the only ones left at the table when I walked in. Audrey was sitting with an empty plate, but Carl was still eating.

"Are you a slow eater, or is that your third burger?" I asked with a chuckle.

"You are on a need-to-know basis, sir," Carl said with his mouth full.

"Oh, that is absolutely his third burger," Audrey laughed.

I laughed as I sat down next to Audrey and continued eating my lunch.

"So?" Carl asked.

"Oh, yeah, well, the info he had didn't add much, just more confusion," I replied.

Sam walked back into the room. When he saw me, his eyebrows raised as he waited for me to hit him with the latest update.

"More confusion," Carl said as he reached for more chips.

"Yeah, apparently there is nothing that indicates Max has another job and all, but there have been small amounts of money coming out of my parents' account and into his account for the past few years. I guess he thought if he just took a little at a time, I wouldn't notice since I didn't have a way to check the balance," I said.

Sam's brow furrowed.

"You're the smart one here, Sam, got this one figured out yet?" I asked.

"I'm working on it," Sam replied.

Joe walked into the room as we were all thinking. "Goodness, it is quiet in here. I don't think any of you worked this hard at problem-solving while you were still in school! Anyways, I thought it would be better if you took the truck. It has a covered extended bed. Sam said the storage unit had a decent amount of supplies, and the more we can get per trip, the better. Sam, you think you'd be okay driving that thing?"

Sam squinted at his dad and smirked. "If mom can drive it, then I can drive it."

"You have a point, son," Joe said.

"I heard that!" yelled Mila from the kitchen.

Joe's eyebrows shot up, and his mouth stretched as he breathed through his teeth. "Yikes, I'm in trouble now!"

"No dessert for you!" Mila shouted back.

"Did somebody say dessert?" Carl asked, standing from his chair and looking around the room for signs of something sweet.

Mila came in from the kitchen with bags hooked on her arm and a tray of cookies in her hand. "Here," she said as she handed the bags to Sam. "There is dinner in there for all of you. I know last time you went down to Seymour you came back starving and smelling like peanut butter." She darted an accusatory glance in Carl's direction.

"Bucket smelled like peanut butter, Mrs. S. He was insistent that I give him the rest of the jar I was eating from," Carl pleaded his case, but Mila knew better.

Mila smiled at Carl. "All the same, I do not want to see you kids go hungry. Not if I can help it."

"Well, you have your work cut out for you with Carl over here," Sam snickered. "Thanks, Mom, love you." Sam kissed his mom on the cheek.

"Wait, what about the cookies?" Joe asked, giving Mila a puppy-dog look.

"Well, I suppose since you helped raise such good boys, you are reprieved from the driving comment," Mila said, smiling. "Help yourselves to some cookies before you leave, and be sure to take some with you for after dinner. There are plenty there."

"You're the best, Mrs. S," Carl said, grabbing a handful of cookies and walking outside.

"Yes, thank you, Mila," Audrey said, as she hugged Mila goodbye.

"Bye, thank you for the dinner and cookies!" I added, as the rest of us walked out to the truck.

"That thing is a gas guzzler, so no car chases this time, please and thank you!" Joe said from the doorway.

The truck was parked on the side of the house. It was a 2004 metallic-sandstone four-wheel-drive Chevy Silverado with an extended bed and cab. I could see why Joe wouldn't want us to go on a wild goose chase with this thing. The truck had been well used but also well taken care of. Sam and Carl let me, Bucket, and Audrey into the back and then climbed in. I let Bucket sit next to the window so he could get some air, and I sat in the middle seat. Sam started up the truck as my phone rang.

"It's Max!" I said with a gasp.

"Well, answer it!" Sam replied.

I placed the phone on speaker. "Hey, Max! You okay, man? We came by your house earlier, and your mom said you were at work, but we stopped by the shop, and you weren't there."

"Oh, yeah, sorry about that. I'm fine. I just met up with my cousin. My mom thinks he is a bad influence, so every time he is in town, I just tell her I'm working. I've been telling her that for years," Max said with a laugh.

I wanted to trust him. It hurt me to know he had been keeping secrets from me, but I still didn't understand why or exactly what. "That's okay, man, I just thought I should ask. Did you get the mark?"

"Scott, man, I didn't want to hide it from you, but I got it a few days ago, right before it became mandatory. I was going to tell you, but you were so caught up with everything at your house, and then when you discovered some of the so-called side effects or whatever you want to call them, I felt ashamed. I regretted the decision but didn't know how to take it back. I was honestly calling to see if there was something you could do to help me."

Sam had backed up the truck and been about to pull out onto the street but stopped to listen more carefully to Max. He turned and looked at me and shrugged his shoulders. None of us knew what to think at this point.

I didn't want to beat around the bush. I wanted answers. "I will do what I can to help you, Max. You know I would do anything for any of you guys. I have to ask you something, though. I was able to look at the bank statements of my parents' account. It looks like money that was in their account somehow got transferred into an account in your name, and I was wondering how and why?"

"I was going to talk to you about that, too. My cousin helped me do it. When I told him that you were my best friend and you weren't taking the mark but I was, he suggested the transfer so that I could still give you access to the money that your parents left you. I didn't want to ask you about it since I hadn't had the time to tell you that I had the mark. That is the exact reason why I called. I wanted to meet up with you and tell you all about it. I hadn't realized you knew about the accounts since you no longer had access to the money anyway. I figured I could do it and it wouldn't hurt anything, and now that I did, we still have access to the funds."

The fact that Max hadn't hesitated before answering made me want to believe him even more. I looked at Carl and Sam for guidance or reassurance, but both gave me looks of bewilderment and shrugged when I raised my eyebrows to silently ask them what I should do.

"Where are you now?" Max continued. "I really want to meet back up with you guys. This way I can talk to you more about it in person."

"Sorry, man, we were just heading to Seymour to pick up some supplies," I started, but Audrey pushed down my hand holding the phone and shook her head. Maybe I shouldn't have told him where we were going, but at least I hadn't given him any specifics. Seymour was a big enough town that I was sure Max would have needed more information to find us, plus Max hadn't gone to the storage unit with us last time.

"Alright, just let me know when you get back, and I'll meet up with you," Max said.

"No problem, just be safe," I replied before hanging up the phone. "Things just keep getting more interesting."

Chapter Seventeen

The ride to Seymour was quiet at first as everyone mulled over the conversation with Max.

"Everything he said seems logical," I said, breaking the silence. "Right?"

"It did to a point, but there are a lot of things that still don't add up," Sam replied. "Like I get what he was saying about the bank account, even though that is beyond sketchy. What doesn't make sense is that there were small amounts taken out years ago before either of you even talked about the mark."

"He had a logical explanation for everything else. It is plausible he has a logical explanation for that and he will tell us later when we meet up. He did say he wanted to talk to me in person, and he answered all the questions I asked. I just didn't ask about that," I replied.

"Maybe, but I still think we need to go into this with the possibility that he may be lying to us," Sam said. "I texted my dad before we left and told him that Max called and knows we are going to Seymour. He seemed a little concerned. It might not be hard to figure out where we are. He knows we went to a storage unit last time we were in Seymour, and there are only, like, three storage unit facilities in Seymour. If he checks each one, this truck is going to stand out."

Audrey looked worried but didn't say anything. I could tell she didn't trust Max, and I could also tell she didn't want to say anything negative about him since she knew he was my friend. I wanted to hold her hand again. I felt awkward. Her hand lay on the seat between us as if she was waiting for me to hold it.

"What do you think?" I asked Audrey.

"It's hard to say," she replied. "At first, I didn't trust him at all, but he did seem to have an answer for everything. The hardest part for me is that there is still someone who betrayed your trust. Someone told the man that broke into your house that you found something. Someone who knew what was in that letter also betrayed you. It seems that Max would be the most likely person to do that, but if you are starting to trust him again, then you need to ask yourself, who else betrayed you?"

Before this, I had thought Detective Clarke had betrayed me, but now I wasn't sure. Either way, I didn't think Max was capable of this kind of technological manipulation on his own, and I was pretty sure his idiot cousin couldn't find his own name in a word search puzzle let alone mastermind a plan like this.

The cab of the truck fell silent again. I stared past Bucket out the window and saw an old boarded-up Texas Roadhouse. My parents used to take me there when I was younger. I could still smell their freshly baked rolls. I missed things like going out to restaurants and taking trips to theme parks. I hadn't done any of those things since my parents had left. I laid my hand on the seat next to me and remembered Audrey's hand was there when my pinky brushed hers.

"Man, oh, man, do I miss the rolls at that place," Carl said exactly what I was thinking. "I can almost smell those rolls now!" Carl took a deep whiff. "Ugh! What is that?"

The rest of us sniffed the air, and the pungent smell hit us all at once.

"Ehhh, it's so gross! I hate the smell of skunk!" Audrey said as she buried her nose into her shirt.

"You know what is worse than the smell of skunk?" Carl asked. "Sam's breath!"

Sam glared at Carl. "Man, I can think of several worse smells than that, and they all come from you, sir."

I laughed while Audrey closed her eyes and shook her head, clearly disapproving of our boyish adolescent bantering.

"Speaking of food, I'm hungry," Carl said. "Where is that bag of food your mom packed for us?"

"Dude, we just ate lunch, like, forty-five minutes ago. This food has to last us through dinner," Sam said with an exasperated sigh.

"Never mind," Carl continued, "I forgot I still had some of those awesome cookies in my pocket!" When he held up a cookie to show off his prized possession to me and Audrey, Bucket snatched it out of Carl's hand and swallowed it whole. Carl jumped in his seat. "No! Not my cookie! Bucket! How could you betray me like that? I'm the one who gave you the peanut butter! Trust me, dog. We are going to have some words later, and I will not be sharing my peanut butter with you anymore!"

Bucket sat high in his seat, panting and seeming to grin, clearly very proud of himself. It made me laugh so hard that everyone else—but Carl—joined in.

"Yeah, yeah, laugh it up," Carl said. "But just know that since he is your dog, I'm taking your cookie as restitution!"

"I mean, seeing as I already ate my cookie, I think I may have to repay you later."

"Dang it!" Carl said, throwing his arms up then folding them across his chest.

"You look like a toddler pouting over, well, a cookie," Sam said as he laughed.

"Alright, you two, "Audrey interrupted. "We have about fifteen more minutes before we get there. I think we should start grabbing supplies as soon as we get there and start loading up the truck. When we get tired and need a break, we can sit down and start looking through the files some more."

"Okay, girl boss," Carl replied.

Audrey smiled smugly, as if she liked being called *girl boss* rather than thought of it as an insult. Her pinky brushed against mine again, and I took that as a sign that I should hold her hand. I placed my hand on top of hers, and her smirk turned into a genuine smile.

The parking lot of the storage facility unit had not changed at all since the last time we had been there except for the addition of some new weeds. I was pretty sure the same trash sat against the fence line, as if the Styrofoam cups were frozen in place in their forever homes.

Sam parked the truck as close to the entry of our unit as possible. This time, Sam had grabbed a flashlight in case the lights decided to go out again. He turned it on despite the fact that we could see just fine.

Halfway to our unit, the lights started to flicker again before one of the screens hanging on the wall in the hallway turned on and started playing an advertisement for the chip. It was creepy, to say the least. I hadn't realized the last time we were here that this place had facial recognition screens or played ads.

The lady with the joker smile urged her audience to get the chip. "Come now and pledge your devotion to our reverent leader, and you, too, can be prosperous."

"That gave me the chills!" Audrey said, placing her face against the sleeve of my shirt.

"That lady reminds me of my fourth-grade teacher. I think I may be getting some PTSD coming on," Carl shivered.

The storage unit was just as we had left it. At least no one had tampered with anything after we had left. Carl grabbed some storage bins from the top shelves and placed them on the floor so Audrey and I could go through them while Sam took inventory for his dad with the notepad and pen he had brought along.

In the storage bins were totes—the first one we looked into full of food—and other items like blankets, medical supplies, and survival kits. Sam logged each item, and we neatly stacked the totes at the front of the storage unit. After we had stacked several totes, we each grabbed one and headed back to the truck. When we passed the monitor, another ad started to play, and Carl jumped in the air and dropped his tote.

"I knew that was going to happen, too! I was waiting for it, and I still jumped," Carl shouted as he gathered his composure and picked back up the tote.

Bucket stayed close to me. I thought he might have been as spooked as Carl.

After we loaded the truck and locked it in case people wandered by looking for supplies to steal out of the units, the ground started to shake. Sam, Carl, and I held onto the side of the truck, and Audrey held onto my arm. Bucket lay on the ground and whimpered. The earthquake seemed to go on longer than usual, and I had to bend down and face the ground as I grew nauseous.

After what seemed like an eternity, the earthquake stopped, and we went back to the storage unit. We made several more trips, and Carl jumped each time we passed the monitors. When most of the totes were in the truck, we started digging through the filing cabinet. Sam sat down at the desk and grabbed a pile of folders while Carl, Audrey, and I sat on the floor eating the dinner Mila had packed for us. Bucket paced back and forth between Sam and the rest of us.

"Anything good yet?" Carl asked.

"Mostly just more of the same crazy stuff we saw the last time. There are lab reports and medical research on some of the projects the company was working on in conjunction with other companies, and it looks like they were even working on some projects to help solve food shortage issues," Sam said as he continued flipping through files.

"Yeah, I'm pretty sure I remember my dad talking about that one. I think that is the major project that my dad headed up. He spent most of his time working on it, and that was all he talked about at home at the dinner table." I felt good remembering my dad's company had worked on some projects that weren't completely unethical.

"Did your dad ever mention the work they were doing with the metaverse? It looks like they were trying to upload digital copies into cyberspace. They started with gameplay but looks like they expanded to virtual worlds and a means of earning an income while living in the metaverse," Sam said.

"Does that mean the digital copy of my brain can work so I don't have to?" Carl asked. "'Cause that would be legit."

"Well, I don't know about that, but I'm pretty sure you need the chip to get your digital copies' earnings, anyway," Sam chuckled.

"I've never heard a lazier question in my life," Audrey said, giving Carl a disappointed look.

"Looks like a key card here," Sam said, holding up a lanyard with a card attached to it.

"Oh, yeah, that looks like the key to my dad's office. I doubt it still works," I replied.

"We should totally go down there and see if we can get into his office. I bet he's got some interesting stuff in there," Carl said.

"I seriously doubt they left his office untouched, but I am kind of curious. If your dad doesn't mind, maybe we can head over there tomorrow after we get all this stuff back to your house," I suggested. "My mom and I used to visit his office from time to time, and no one ever seemed to mind when we came in. We would just go up to the front desk and say we were headed up to Mr. Killian's office, and the receptionist would just smile, and then my mom would use the key card to use the elevator and then again on his office door."

"Okay, I'll text my dad and see if he has other plans for us for tomorrow," Sam said.

Sam continued looking through the files, and Carl laid his head back onto a blanket he had pulled out of one of the totes. I thought this might be a suitable time to talk to Audrey.

"Hey, I'm sorry that Joe embarrassed you earlier when he called you my girlfriend."

"Oh, um, yeah, it's cool. It didn't really bother me," Audrey said as she blushed.

"Oh, good. I kind of hoped it didn't 'cause it's been super cool having you around the last few days and all." I felt like a complete idiot. That wasn't at all what I had wanted to say.

"Oh, okay. Uh, no problem." She seemed slightly irritated by what I had said, or, more likely, by what I hadn't said.

"I guess what I'm trying to say is that I really like you," I managed to blurt out, and Audrey smiled coyly and lowered her head. "I've never had a girlfriend or anything. I mean, there was this one girl, Anna Fikes. She told me I was her boyfriend in kindergarten after she kissed my hand, but then she punched me in the face and gave me a bloody nose, so, yeah, I didn't figure that one counted."

Audrey stifled a laugh, and it came out as a snort. "Well, I promise to never punch you in the face."

"That is a huge relief! I didn't know exactly where this conversation would go, but I can safely say that I can now define our relationship as a commitment to not punch each other in the face. Which, for the record, is the best commitment I have had in my life because I definitely wouldn't be surprised if Carl decked me in the face for a cheeseburger."

Audrey laughed, and I started to turn my head toward Carl, who appeared to be fast asleep on the floor, but before I could face him completely, Audrey leaned in and kissed me on the lips. It didn't last long, but I knew I would never forget this moment. I reached up to brush a stray hair from her face and tucked it behind her ear when Bucket started to whimper.

"What is it, Bucket?" Sam asked, placing down the folders on the desk.

I hit Carl's foot to wake him up and stood so I could be closer to the unit's door, which was closed. "I hear footsteps," I whispered.

"Well, I don't think there is a need to panic. I'm sure there are still people who use this place regularly," Sam whispered back.

As the sound of footsteps grew closer, we could hear the approaching person attempting to open unit doors. It sounded like a few of them opened and then were shut again, as if the person hadn't found what they were looking for.

"Someone could have seen the truck and came in here to look for us," Audrey whispered.

Just then, the ad in the hallway came on, and we all jumped. "Do you have what it takes to lead people into the future? Join the One World governance today, and see how you can make a difference!"

It had to be someone that had the mark; those ads only played for people who were chipped.

"We should turn off the lights and hold the door down so when they come by, they don't see a light shining through," I suggested.

Sam turned off the lights, and we all pushed down on the door, hoping that when the person came by our unit, they would assume it was locked. I could hear my breathing getting faster and louder. I tried to slow it down, fearing the person on the other side of the door would hear it.

After taking a few more steps, the stranger stopped in front of our unit. They grunted a little as they tried to lift the door. After a few seconds, they gave up, and the steps continued onto the next unit.

"What should we do?" I whispered to Sam. "If we stay put, eventually that person will walk back and wait us out by the truck."

"You're right," Sam whispered back. "I think we should wait till whoever that is is at the end of this row, and then we make a run for it to the truck."

"That might not work since the truck only has two doors, so we would have to be climbing in over each other. By the time we all got in the truck, that person could already be in their car and block us at the entrance, or worse, we could end up in another car chase, and I don't think your truck is going anywhere fast with all those supplies loading it down," I said.

Sam started to reply, but then we heard the storage facility's entrance door open.

Almost immediately after that, a voice came from the direction opposite the entrance—from, I guessed, the person who had just passed us. "Scott, it's me! I know you guys are here. Where are you?"

It was Max.

Chapter Eighteen

Without thinking, I pulled up on the storage unit door.

"Scott! Don't!" Sam said in a loud whisper, but it was too late.

The door was open, and Max stared down at us from the end of the hallway. I quickly turned toward the entrance, but whomever had come in moments ago must have turned around and left when they heard voices. I instinctively had my arms out, blocking Sam and Audrey from coming out into the hallway in case it wasn't safe.

"Max, man, you scared us. What are you doing here?" I asked him, having to shout down the hall.

"I wanted to meet up with you and talk to you, remember?" Max replied.

"Long way to go just to talk," I yelled back. Neither of us had taken a step toward the other. "How did you find us?"

"I stopped at another storage unit around town first. When I didn't see anyone there, I headed here and saw the truck," Max replied.

I looked at Sam.

He rolled his eyes and mumbled under his breath, "Bro, I told you."

"Someone with you?" I asked. I realized we must have been hearing two sets of footsteps, as Max didn't drive, and the bus wouldn't just drive him around to different storage units.

I took a step forward while Carl, Sam, and Audrey remained hidden in the unit and put my hands out to show they were empty—not that I ever would have hurt Max, but he looked a little frazzled.

"No, just me," Max yelled back as he took a step forward.

A lump grew in my throat. This was the first time I didn't believe something Max said to me. "How'd you get here, man?"

Max froze. We both stared at each other, and after a moment, I took two steps back. I looked at Audrey and nodded for her to leave behind me. Sam and Carl stepped out of the unit after her, and Sam shut the door. I kept my gaze on Max the entire time.

"I loved you like a brother," I yelled to Max.

Max still didn't move or say anything as I took a few more steps backward.

"You're breaking my heart, Max. Whatever you are caught up in, you don't have to do it. We will help you. All of us."

"There's so much you don't know, Scott. I'm not here to hurt you. I want what's best for you, too, but you can't keep living the way you are living. You need to get the chip, otherwise, you are going to be running for the rest of your life. You have the chance to be very successful, and I can help you, not the other way around." Max's words cut me like a knife.

I took a few more steps back. "We showed you what that mark is about, Max. We showed you the proof that you can't trust it or the companies responsible for giving it. You can't trust Gabby Gabe. Making things easy for yourself for a moment isn't going to be worth the end result." With every word that came out of my mouth, I took another step backward. Carl, Sam, and Audrey were already waiting at the storage facility's entrance.

"I know the truth, Scott. I need to show you. You don't know what you are talking about. Come with us, and we can show you," Max said as he took a step forward.

"Us, Max? Who's us?" I was at the entrance door at this point but hesitated to walk out.

"The man that's been following you, Scott. The one in your house that night. He doesn't want to hurt you. We both want to help you."

My heart sank. I didn't want to give up on Max, but we needed to get to the truck. I turned away from Max and grabbed the handle of the entrance door. It flung open, and I could see the same car that had chased us that night from my house.

"Get to the truck!" I yelled at everyone. We ran to the truck, but when we opened the truck's doors, I heard a voice behind me.

"Scott, are you guys okay?"

I turned to see Detective Clarke. "Max is inside. He told me everything," I responded.

"What are you talking about? Everything about what?" Clarke sounded sincerely confused.

"We know it was you that chased us from our house that night," I said.

"Scott, what are you talking about? I'm friends with Sam's dad, Joe. He texted me after you guys left when Sam told him that Max called you. He was worried about you guys and asked if I would check up on you."

Before I could react, a man came up behind Clarke and hit him over the head with what looked like a crowbar. Clarke dropped to his knees, and then his body fell forward to the ground. Blood oozed from his head onto the gravel.

My eyes widened, and my heart raced. Sam, the only one in the truck, started it up as Carl let out a blood-curdling scream. Bucket whimpered and put his face into my leg while Audrey grabbed my arm and hid her face in the same manner. Standing in front of us was the tall man with the Colts hat, dark sunglasses, and long dark jacket. Behind him, the door to the storage unit opened, and Max stood in the doorway.

This was the closest I had ever been to the man who had been following me, and I sensed an uneasy familiarity about him. I stood still for a second longer than I should have, trying to get a better look at the man's face despite the fact that I was terrified by what had just happened.

"Scott! Let's get out of here, man!" Carl grabbed my arm and yanked me toward the truck.

"Do you think Clarke is dead?" I asked, but I didn't know whom I was talking to.

I climbed in the truck after Audrey, then Carl jumped in and slammed the door. Audrey was breathing heavily. I wasn't sure if she was hyperventilating or trying not to cry. My head was spinning. Sam peeled out of the gravel drive and onto the road. I looked back, but the man and Max were not following us. They were sitting in their car as if their car wouldn't start.

"Do you think Clarke is dead?" I asked again. My eyes filled with tears for both Max and Clarke. "How could he do this to me? To us?"

"Max made his own decision, and we can't know or understand it, but it seems to me he made it a long time ago." Sam spoke calmly, but his hands were clenched tightly around the steering wheel. "As for Clarke, I hope he is okay. I think we should call nine-one-one and tell them anonymously what happened."

"I got it," Carl said, pulling out his phone.

While Carl talked to dispatch, I leaned closer to Audrey. "Are you okay?"

She nodded, but I could tell she was too shaken up to talk. I put my arm around her and held her close to me, and she started to cry.

"It's okay to cry. I kind of feel like crying myself right now," I said. "I think now may be a perfect time to pray." I had never prayed out loud with anyone but my parents before. Audrey nodded, and we both bowed our heads and began to pray for Clarke.

Carl was still on the phone with dispatch. "They said there was an officer just down the road and he was heading there right now, and they want me to hold."

"Put it on speaker," Sam said.

Carl put the phone on speaker, and we heard a voice come through in a matter of seconds. "The officer is at the facility. He says there is no body and no car, but there was some blood on the gravel. Can you give me your information?"

Carl's eyes grew wide. He looked at Sam and said, "Uhhh my name is Max, Max Lambert," then hung up the phone.

"If there was no car, then Detective Clarke's car wasn't there either," Audrey suggested.

"Maybe Max drove his car with Clarke's body inside." Carl rocked back and forth in his seat. "How are we going to find out if he is okay?"

"Why don't you try calling him?" Sam said with exasperation.

"Oh, yeah, why didn't I think of that?" Carl dialed Clarke's number.

After the second ring, Clarke picked up. "Carl, you guys okay?" He sounded groggy.

"Oh man, are we glad to hear your voice! We thought you were gone, man!" Carl said as he flopped himself back into his seat and let his free hand fall by his side with relief.

"I feel blessed right now. The way he hit me took a chunk of skin off the bone, and I was bleeding pretty bad, but I've managed to stop the bleeding, and so far, it seems my brain is intact."

When Clarke said he felt blessed, I wondered if he was a Christian as well. He had mentioned he was friends with Joe, and I started to feel horrible for accusing him of being the guy who was chasing us.

"I'm sorry I thought you were the one working with Max. I knew he was with someone, so when I came out and saw you, I just assumed." My apology felt weak considering he had been seriously hurt trying to help us.

"Don't worry about it, Scott," Clarke said reassuringly. "I'm just glad you guys are okay. When I came to, both of your cars were gone, so I didn't know what happened. I have a friend who can stitch me up, but I think we better tell Joe that getting everyone to my shelter is our next priority."

"*Your* shelter?" I asked, surprised.

"Yeah, I wanted to keep things rather hushed because I didn't know which people I could trust just yet. I think you boys are proving yourselves quite well. Sorry it had to be under these types of circumstances."

Sam must have known and not told us so he wouldn't betray Clarke's trust.

"After I get my head checked out, I'll head to Joe's. He has a trailer there loaded and ready for me to haul it with my truck back to the hideout," Clarke continued.

"I know this is going to sound like a terrible idea, but after we drop this stuff off at the shelter tomorrow, I think we may head up to my dad's old office at KTI. I just feel like there are some pieces to the puzzle we don't have yet, and I want to see if my dad's old key card will still let me in to look around. Maybe I can even find out who is behind all this."

"Uh, yeah, that does in fact sound like a terrible idea," Clarke responded. "But I wouldn't stop you. God has definitely used you in some mysterious ways, and if you feel like you are being led to do this, then you probably should. But I would absolutely pray about it first. It's a good thing you have some amazing friends."

Praying about decisions was something new to me, but I didn't want to make big decisions on my own anymore, and I was glad Clarke agreed.

"We'll see you later, man, glad you are okay!" Sam said, leaning toward the phone while he drove. "I'm glad I don't have to tell my dad that I'm responsible for getting one of his best friends killed."

"Ha! Joe knows how thick-headed I can be, and this just proves it," Clarke responded. "I'll catch up with you boys later. Be safe, and God be with you."

"I still think my dad is going to freak out a little when I tell him what happened tonight, not to mention what my mom's reaction is going to be," Sam said after Clarke hung up. "But anyways, I guess now's as good a time as any to bring up the elephant in the room, so to speak—so, uh, Max, huh?"

"Dude, my boy has been there for me through thick and thin, and now he is just going to play us like that. I just don't get it." Carl looked uncharacteristically angry.

"Honestly, I don't think he thought he was doing anything wrong," I started, and Carl looked back at me, his wide eyes insinuating I was crazy. "I think he has been deceived and truly thinks that he can help us. I think he wants us to go on the same as we always have, living normal lives by going to work and hanging out. I think he thinks the only way we can do that is if we give up the faith and get the chip. This way we, our group, can be normal again. He doesn't see the wrong in what he is doing."

"That man grabbed a metal bar, a metal bar I tell you, and whacked Clarke across the head, probably trying to kill the man, and you're going to tell me that 'he doesn't see the wrong he is doing'?" Carl made quotation marks in the air as he repeated my words.

"I saw the look on his face when Clarke was hit. He looked upset," I replied.

"Do you see this look?" Carl turned in his seat to face me and pointed to his face. "This is what upset looks like! I saw blood!"

Sam snickered. "It's not funny, but I can't help but laugh at the idea of you becoming a cop. I can just picture you showing up for a nine-one-one call and then screaming like a girl when you see blood."

Carl sniffed. "Oh, it's like that?"

Audrey laughed, and it made me feel good that she had stopped crying even if it was only for a moment.

I laughed as well. "Sorry, man, but he's not lying," I said as I patted Carl on the back.

Carl knew full well he couldn't argue with Sam's statement. "Yeah, well, I'm Mila's favorite, so there."

Sam laughed. "Yeah, I'll give you that one. I'm pretty sure you are."

Carl nodded in approval of his small victory.

"In all seriousness, though, I don't want to give up on Max. I want to find him and help him and find out who has been twisting his mind around," I said.

"My dad talks about getting the mark as a final decision kind of thing," Sam said, looking back at me in the rearview mirror. "I understand where you are coming from, but I just don't want you to get your hopes up, but I'll help you any way I can. We are family. We are all family."

Getting back to Sam's house was a huge relief. Joe was excited about the list of supplies that Sam gave him, but he said he didn't think making another trip to the storage unit was worth putting us at risk. We all helped Joe and Nate load up the rest of the boxes he had stacked in the living room onto the trailer he had parked out back.

"We can all go to the shelter tomorrow and unload all these supplies," Joe started. "So far it looks like we are doing surprisingly well. I just wish we had a backup generator and maybe some more water. You can never have enough water."

"Oh! I have a generator at my house," I exclaimed. "I saw one at the store and thought that it would be cool to have even if I didn't know why or when I would need one. I think there's more five-gallon jugs of water and canned food at home we couldn't fit in Sam's car, too."

Joe threw up his arms. "What? And you didn't tell me?"

"I'm telling you right now," I said with a chuckle.

"Okay, well, I am going to swing by your house and pick that up in the morning on the way out if you don't mind."

"Not at all. I can give you the key, and you can do a sweep of the house to see if there is anything else you would like to grab. I'm sure there are a handful of things I haven't told you about yet because I didn't know you wanted them," I said as I picked up another box.

I walked out to the truck with the box and passed Audrey making her way back into the house. I smiled and winked at her as I passed by. I had never winked at anyone before, so I felt awkward as soon as I did it, but she smiled and blushed in return.

After we grabbed the rest of the boxes and loaded them in the trailer, we all went to our respective beds for the night. I prayed, thanking God for keeping us safe and protecting Detective Clarke. I asked for guidance about going to my dad's office, then I prayed for Max, though that was more difficult. I loved him like a brother, but I didn't know if I would ever be his friend again. It was hard to think that he was lost even though it wasn't long ago I had been lost myself.

Chapter Nineteen

I woke up Monday to the rain beating against the roof of the house. It was dark out, but the morning sun was peeking through the dreary clouds. We had gone so long without rain, and now it seemed continuous. I grabbed my Bible and headed to the kitchen, as if my reading would disturb Carl. I had been reading for a half hour before I heard anyone else in the house get up. Mila was the first one to walk into the kitchen.

"Scott, I wasn't expecting to see you up so early. I was just about to get breakfast started. Are you hungry?"

"For something you make? I am always hungry," I replied with a grin.

"Joe and Nate are going to head to your house this morning before everyone else takes off to go to the shelter. I figured they would be up before you," Mila said as she pulled eggs out of the refrigerator.

"I couldn't sleep. I just keep thinking about Max and wondering if there is anything I can do to help him. Sam said that since he got the mark that it may be too late. Is that true?" I asked.

"Scott, all I can tell you is what the Bible says. I know that the Gospels say the only unforgivable sin is blasphemy or rejection of the Holy Spirit. I guess if taking the mark is a form of blasphemy against the Holy Spirit, then that is the path Max chose. I just don't know, and I don't have all the answers. I think all you can do at this point is pray. Pray for wisdom, peace, and understanding. These next few years are going to be the hardest we have ever had to deal with. People are going to persecute us, and our lives are going to be in constant jeopardy."

I nodded. These were things my mom had warned me about as well. I felt sad because of Max's choices, but I felt humble and thankful that God had found me despite myself and my own choices. I was thankful that my mother had thought to leave behind things that could help others, like myself, during this time. I was thankful for having great friends and having Joe and Mila take me in as one of their own and teach me the truths about God's Word. Without thinking, I bowed my head and praised God for all He had provided for me and for His divine intervention that I had witnessed this week.

Mila came close to me, placed her hand on my back, and bowed her head. She didn't pray out loud, but I knew she was praying for me at that moment. Only a few moments passed before Joe walked into the kitchen.

"Nate and Sam are going out back now to gather eggs and milk. As soon as we eat, Nate and I will head to Scott's house to pick up the generator and other supplies."

"Do they need any help?" I asked.

"Stay put, I'm about to whip you up an amazing omelet," Mila replied.

It seemed like as soon as I grabbed my plate, everyone flooded into the kitchen all at once.

"What is going on in here?" Carl asked. "I sleep in just a few minutes, and everyone starts eating without me. You should all know that I prioritize my food over sleep every time."

Audrey chuckled. "You should also know that Scott was the first one up. He was even up before Bucket this morning, and Bucket eats almost as much as you do, Carl."

"Oh, yeah," I jumped in, "that reminds me. Joe, I have some dog food still at my house. It is in the kitchen by the back door, if you could grab that for Bucket. I'm sure he would appreciate it. There is quite a bit there because I stocked up last time I was at the store. I think there may be some more detergent bottles in that side pantry too that we forgot. I had so many that I started placing them wherever I could find an empty spot."

"Well, that will make Bucket and the misses very happy for sure," Joe said, wiggling his eyebrows up and down at Mila. I wasn't sure what that look was supposed to mean, but Mila laughed.

Joe started writing the directions to the shelter on a piece of paper. "Sam, here are the directions. You need to make sure that you take this side road here one mile after you turn right onto Mulberry Way. It isn't on the map, but we had some guys make some side roads through the woods to prevent anyone from tracking our cars. Before you get on this road, you will need to remove the on-board unit from the truck. Oh, and don't use GPS in any capacity. We don't want anyone to be able to locate the shelter unless we want them there, so make sure to turn off all cell phones before getting on the side road."

"Got it," Sam said as he took the keys. He tossed them into the air to try and catch them with the same hand, but Carl snatched them before Sam could.

"Oh, son, you're going to have to be quicker than that," Carl said to Sam as he tossed back his keys.

"Let's roll," Sam said, shaking his head at Carl.

We all piled in the truck and took off for the shelter. It was a nice drive through the countryside. We passed a lot of abandoned farmhouses and several of what appeared to be ghost towns, around which we spotted only a few people. We also saw a lot of cats wandering around the small towns. Bucket enjoyed sticking his head out the window and occasionally barking at the cats.

"Should only be a few more miles before we need to pull over and take the OBU off this thing," Sam said. "My dad said there was an old mailbox that we could stick it in until we started to head back."

We pulled over, took off the OBU, then walked to some brush that was blocking a road. Audrey transitioned into the driver's seat as Carl, Sam, and I pulled the brush away from the path. We waited for Audrey to pull the truck through then covered the path's opening back up with the brush before heading the rest of the way to the shelter.

We drove down a rough gravel-and-dirt road through the woods until we hit an opening. From there, we could see a large building that resembled a school. As we drove closer, we could see people unloading lumber into the building. We drove up close to the door, and Detective Clarke was the first person we saw as he walked outside onto the front step. He was wearing blue jeans and a gray t-shirt, which seemed to have manifested the same yellow mustard stain that usually donned his white button-up. He held up his hand to signal we could stop where we were and approached the truck.

"It's good to see you boys again!" Clarke exclaimed. "After I blacked out, my head went in a lot of different directions as to what could have happened next."

"I think we are more relieved to see you," Sam replied. "How's your head doing?"

"Only four stitches, if you can believe that. Either that guy had a weak arm, or I had a guardian angel pulling it back. In my line of work, I've seen guys get hit with a lot less and have a lot more trauma, that's for sure."

Sam threw the truck into park and turned off the ignition. "Is it okay to park here to unload this thing?"

"Yeah, I'll have some guys come out and help you in a minute. For now, let me show you all around the place," Clarke said.

"Sounds good," Sam said as he jumped out of the truck, quickly followed by Bucket. "This is Inspector Bucket, since you two haven't been formally introduced."

Clarke squatted down in front of Bucket. "Ah, Chief Inspector Bucket. That makes you my boss! But I suspect you are everyone's boss around here," he said as he rubbed Bucket's head. "I have a feeling we are going to be good friends. Come on, let's go take a tour."

We headed toward the old red-brick building. It was in good shape, but the years had faded the color of the brick on the side not shielded by the trees. Weeds had sprouted up throughout the grounds, and the parking lot was filled with cracks through which grass and more weeds grew.

Inside was a small foyer that led to a front desk, which stood in front of several offices. To the left and right of the entrance were hallways. The floor was made of cream and light blue tiles. Despite their old appearance, they seemed to be in good shape. We turned left from the entrance down the hall, and after about twenty feet, the hallway turned right to reveal a row of blue lockers and doors to classrooms.

"We have been working on transforming the classrooms into what would look more like dorm rooms," Clarke stated as he pointed to the first room we came across on our left. "This is one that we have finished."

Inside, the classroom still had a dry-erase board on the wall but was otherwise more like a dorm room. It contained three sets of bunk beds, dressers, and a mirror, and in the center over the gray carpet was a cream-colored area rug on which sat a couch and a coffee table.

"I know it doesn't look like much, but we have been trying to make the best use of the space we have," Clarke said. "There is even a TV in here so we can keep an eye on the news updates. All the electronics we brought in are older so we can make sure nothing is tracking us here."

"How do you have electricity?" Audrey asked.

"The building was already set up with solar panels when my grandfather bought the place three years ago," Clarke replied. "After everyone disappeared, the school lost so many teachers that it just went down. The building was sold at an auction for dirt cheap, and my grandfather bought it right before he passed away. I'm not sure what he was planning on doing with it, but since it was left to me, I started turning it into a backup shelter from the beginning. I never knew it would turn into this, though. Anyway, to continue answering your question, I took the solar panels off my house and added them to the building, increasing the amount of energy the building can store. It also has a well so we can keep off of the grid although we need to bottle up some more water to save. This area wasn't hit with that water that killed so many people, but we also need to prepare for the future, and I don't trust that the water is going to stay safe."

"How do you watch TV?" Sam asked. "Wouldn't having the internet show our location?"

"Yeah, normally it would," Clarke responded. "But we know a guy that has been able to use the abandoned satellites in space to provide the internet to us without anyone being able to follow a trace or location. It's pretty genius but definitely not my field of expertise. Owen seems to be the best of the best."

"Owen?" I asked with excitement. "A guy named Owen helped our video go viral!"

"Sounds like the same Owen to me, but you should be able to see for yourself. He should be by here later this morning," Clarke replied.

We walked out of the room and toward the back of the hall, passing other rooms that were set up similarly to the first. The lockers were in decent shape, and the smell of Pine-Sol permeated the halls. Carl grabbed a locker door to see if it would open, and it did. Inside was empty and clean.

"Sweet, this one's open. Dibs," Carl said. "I never had a locker before. We had some in our school, but they stopped using them years before we started high school."

"As a matter of fact, they are all open," Clarke replied, smiling at Carl's excitement. "We figured we could use them for extra storage and coat closets and such. At the end of the hallway was the old home-ec room, which we tried to make it a little homier. There is basically a full kitchen set up in there as well as sewing machines and tons of craft items. They were all left behind by the school."

"Hopefully, the fridge is not like the fridge I have at my house because that thing could track us better than my phone," I said, laughing.

We arrived at the end of the hall, and Clarke pointed left.

"If you head down that way, you will see the locker rooms, stage, cafeteria, and gymnasium. Most of those we have left untouched, but we did try to make the locker rooms a bit nicer since we will most likely be using them for showers. There are plenty of other restrooms in the school, but the only showers are down there. We stuck some cabinets down there and put in a bunch of essentials like soap, shampoo, and towels. Oh, and don't worry, we made sure to have plenty of deodorant." Clarke raised his eyebrows at us at his last comment.

"Don't look at me," Carl said with his arms in the air. "I smell fresh!" Carl turned his head toward his own armpit and took a big whiff. His smile turned into a scowl with squinted eyes and a scrunched-up his nose. He wafted the smell away with his hand. "Okay, I lied. I smell like Sam."

Sam jabbed Carl's arm. The rest of us couldn't help but laugh.

"Hey!" Carl grabbed his arm as if in pain. "It's not my fault I had to use your soap and deodorant the past few days. I think this scent is called 'Sasquatch in the Wild' or something."

"The ladies love it," Sam said, laughing.

We all immediately turned toward Audrey.

"Hey, don't look at me," Audrey said. "I'm not getting anywhere near those pits to tell you if that's true or not. What I will say is that it does sometimes get a little stinky on those long car rides, but I'm not pointing any fingers."

Instinctively, Sam and I both sniffed our own armpits to make sure it wasn't one of us. Relieved to know it wasn't me, I looked down at Bucket. "Do you need a bath, boy?"

We all laughed and continued to follow Clarke down the next hallway on the right.

"This room used to be the school's chapel, and we pretty much kept it that way. We have chairs set up in there, but there are also some foosball tables, ping pong tables, and some board games and stuff in the back. We also took any instruments that were left in the music room and brought them down here as well. We may be able to make a joyful noise but not sure how pleasant it will sound!" Clarke chuckled.

We rounded the corner, took another right, and found ourselves in another long hallway of blue lockers and classrooms.

"In this hallway, we have the rooms set up more like family units. We have been doing the most work in this area, putting up walls and setting up the classrooms to fit families a bit better. We also have some toy boxes with toys that are more appropriate for grade-school children, and we have one room left that is set up like a classroom where we can conduct school."

"This place is amazing!" Sam said, reaching out to shake Clarke's hand.

"I can't take the credit," Clarke said, shaking Sam's hand. "I had the place, but the brains and setup were done by other people, and your dad was a huge help in all of this."

We walked back toward the entrance, coming full circle, then turned right around the corner to an office.

"There were a few offices here, so we set up one of them as a small library. We took all the leftover books from the original library and brought them in here along with any Bibles we could get our hands on. We turned another office into a computer room. It has a lot of high-tech stuff that I'm pretty sure I'd get my hands slapped if I tried to touch. Owen has a setup in there, and I think there are more TV screen monitors than there were on my entire block back home."

"I would love to learn from him," Audrey said excitedly. "Before I started working with cars, I was trying to learn more about computers. It took a back seat when I had to make a living for myself, but I did learn from some of my friends. Even Russell taught me a few things."

"I'm sure we could use you. It is a smart idea to have more than one person learn each task around here. The more people who know how to do each task, the better," Clarke responded.

"I'll be happy to volunteer with any construction work that needs to be done," I added. "My grandfather taught me a lot, and I've been pretty handy at the house the past few years without any help. Where would you like us to unload the totes from the truck? We also have our personal items, too."

"You boys can take your personal stuff to that first room we looked at. None of those bunks have been claimed yet. Audrey, there is a room across the hall and two doors down from the boys' room that you can put your stuff in. There are two gals already in there, and they can show you which beds are available."

A tear had welled up in the corner of Audrey's eye as she reached toward Clarke on her tiptoes and gave him a big hug. "Thank you! You have no idea what this means to me."

Clarke seemed taken aback at first but then smiled and hugged her back. "You all mean a lot to me, too." Clarke looked up at someone coming around the corner. "Speaking of roommates."

Carl's Aunt Aniyah came rushing toward Carl to give him a hug.

"I've been worried sick about you!" Aniyah said.

"You've been worried about me? I've been worried about you! I hadn't heard from you, I didn't know what happened to you," Carl replied.

"I know, I'm so sorry. I got arrested."

"Arrested? You're, like, this sweet old lady."

"Carl Jeffrey Williamson! If you call me a sweet old lady again, I will bend you over my knee!" They both laughed, but I was sure his aunt was only half joking. "I was caught continuing my business. I was trading for food, and since I didn't have the chip implant, they said I was evading taxes and stuff. Luckily, Clarke still has connections and was able to pick me up from the precinct. I just got here late last night."

"I'm glad to see you, too," I said.

"Oh, you boys don't have to worry about me. I accepted the Lord, and I am ready when He is. I just don't want to wear a prison jumpsuit, so unflattering, I would have to alter that thing. They have some sewing machines in the back here, though, so anyone that needs any clothes or alterations, you just bring them to me, and I will take care of it. I don't want anyone here to feel like they are stuck wearing something they hate."

"Ha, alright, Aunty, I won't worry about you anymore. You just worry about making everyone here look good and feel comfortable."

Chapter Twenty

We unloaded the totes from the truck and took them through a different doorway, which led to the gymnasium. We stacked all the supplies on the gym's stage. The gym's lights made a buzzing sound, and the place looked dark even after we turned on all the lights. Someone said the lights were warming up. On the stage were already tons of cardboard boxes, milk crates, and totes full of supplies in separate piles.

We were setting down some totes on the front of the stage when a lady came around the side entrance and joined us. She held a clipboard and wore a blue V-neck t-shirt and jeans. She was probably in her mid-thirties with long dark hair and looked a lot like Mila. Her face was beaming with joy.

"Sam! Come here, you! I am so glad you boys made it here safe!"

"Aunt Talia!" Sam threw his arms around the woman. "My mom didn't tell me you were here! Guys, this is my mom's sister Talia."

We all shook hands, said hello, and introduced ourselves.

"I wanted to surprise you! I accepted the Lord as my Savior two months ago. Since then, Mila has been insistent that I come here. I finally packed up the truck twelve days ago and drove straight here from Newark. I've been helping Joe with inventory, but I told him not to tell you I was here until I saw you so I could surprise you. Then I heard you kept running into trouble. Clarke said he was going to make sure you guys were okay and then came back with stitches. And I thought Newark was getting bad!" she said with a nervous laugh.

"I haven't been this excited in a long time," Sam said as he hugged her again. "It feels like Christmas. So happy to hear you got saved. Mom told me when it happened. She was crying for a day straight; she was so happy. I can't believe she was able to keep you coming here a secret."

She squeezed him tightly, mussed his hair, then turned to Audrey. "I think that we are going to be bunkmates!"

Audrey practically jumped into Talia's arms to hug her. "I've always wanted a sister, and now I have one!"

The sight of them hugging made me smile. Sometimes I forgot that other people were lonelier than I'd been. Audrey had a tough exterior, but her softness on the inside drew me closer to her.

Talia pulled her clipboard back up to her face and looked at the list. "Joe gave me a copy of the items that you brought. Food items can go toward the back of the stage. Toiletries can go stage left, and all other items, for now, can go stage right. We already have a van full of people heading here from Ohio tomorrow. They are coming with only the clothes on their backs, so we will need to start distributing a lot of the supplies soon. We are also anticipating more groups as the word spreads. There are many small Christian groups that are being forced from their homes or are in desperate need of food."

"Alright, well, let's get the rest of them supplies then!" Carl said as he jumped off the stage and started to head toward the truck.

Sam jumped off the stage behind Carl, and the two of them raced to the truck. I walked to the stairs left of the stage and walked down with Audrey. By the time I arrived at the truck, another car came into view from the road in the woods. It was a black Mustang. I helped unload more totes from the truck but stayed outside for Owen. He pulled up close to the truck and stepped out of the car.

"Good morning," I yelled out.

"Scott," he said with a nod. He leaned on the side of his car and pulled out his tin. This time, he pulled out a stick of gum before presenting me with the tin. It had been a while since I had chewed gum, so I grabbed one from the tin and popped it into my mouth.

"Quit smoking?" I asked.

"Yeah, well, I figured there were going to be plenty of opportunities to die and things that could kill me, so why not eliminate this one? Let something else kill me."

"I suppose that's as good a reason as any."

"So how have you been?" Owen asked.

"Yeah, so my friend that somehow got ahold of my money has been working with the guy that has been following me and broke into my house, so there's that. Oh, and that friend of his clocked Clarke over the head with a crowbar."

"Ouch, nice friend. Yeah, Clarke mentioned the bump. Sorry I was the one that had to break the news to you about Max," Owen replied. "I'm sure you guys were close. I've lost a few close friends in the last couple of years as well. People became super political, and all of a sudden it was no longer okay for me to be more of the anarcho-capitalist type that they thought was cool in the past."

"So how did you manage to hook up with this group of people here?" I asked.

Owen pulled out another stick of gum and popped it into his mouth before he answered. I could tell the habit of constantly putting something into his mouth would take a while to change. "Clarke and I go way back. He was a good cop, but he didn't always like the directive he was to follow. He thought the force was there to protect and serve the people, and his boss thought it was to control and discipline the people. He and I would go out for coffee from time to time and talk politics and religion. Then he changed. His negative perspective on life became positive. His hate for his boss turned to forgiveness. I wasn't quite there yet, but we continued to meet up. After I helped upload that video of yours, we talked again, and that's when I started to turn around myself. I'm still a work in progress, but I like the direction. So what's next for you?"

"I still feel like I'm missing something," I replied while looking around the grounds, as if the missing puzzle piece might be here. "I want to try to go into my dad's old office and see if he left anything there. It seems like my dad's company had a bigger hand in everything we are fighting against than I thought was possible. My parents started to pull and hide some of that information so I could find it, but I still feel like there is more. I have an old key card that I'm hoping will still work and let us in the office."

"The company most likely only uses the chip now to open the doors." Owen was immediately in his element. "They are similar to key cards in that they use RFID, and it's hard to bypass the RFID security without the right tools. Luckily, I have the right tools. In the office, they probably have a pretty standard system that uses electrical signals sent through wires through the electronic chip in their hand. As long as the chip belongs to an authorized employee, the door will open. I think I can have my computer interact with the key-card reader and then pull all that information out as well and then program a master key card."

"Sounds to me like you're just the guy I need for this job," I replied.

"I would love to come with you if you have the room. I may be able to do some damage while I'm on their computers," Owen said with a maniacal snicker that made me laugh.

"I'll talk to Sam, I'm sure we can create a team!" I replied, laughing and shaking my head at Owen's joy in cyber-attacking.

"That Barts woman in charge over there is no joke, either. And speaking of Barts, I noticed that some items purchased from transactions made from your account were delivered straight to her home address. So she may be deeply involved with whoever is working with Max."

"Well, it makes sense that someone with power was working with Max and not just his idiot cousin. Just don't know what she would want with me unless she knew my parents hid the information about the company for me and wanted to stop me." I patted Owen on the shoulder. "Thanks again for the heads up. It may have saved us back at the storage unit."

I made my way back to the truck and grabbed another tote to bring into the gym, and Owen followed suit.

"This is Owen, he is the one who helped us upload our video," I said to the group standing on the stage with Talia. I put the tote on the stage and pointed at each person as I said their name. "Sam, Carl, Audrey, Talia, and that is Inspector Bucket."

"I actually know Talia. We met a couple days ago, and believe it or not, I also know Inspector Bucket. I thought that looked like him when I came in," Owen said as he put down his tote and squatted to the ground. "Come here, boy."

Bucket ran to Owen and looked overjoyed, spinning in circles as Owen ran his hands all over his fluffy coat.

"I think he likes you!" I said.

"His owner was an old buddy of mine. I often wondered what happened to this guy. Glad to see he is in good hands now." Owen stuck out his finger like a gun. "Bang!" Bucket fell down and played dead. "Good boy, Bucket! You still got it!"

"Wow, what other tricks does he do?" Carl asked.

"Oh, this guy has an entire repertoire," Owen replied.

"I believe it," Carl added. "I've seen him in action."

"So not to shift the attention off Bucket or anything, but Owen and I were talking about going up to my dad's office to look around. Owen said he can get us in even if this key card I have is outdated. I know we planned on going up there today, but it looks like there is a lot to do here. I think we can give Owen time to get what he needs, and we can go first thing tomorrow morning."

"I think that is a good idea," Audrey replied. "But I think I will sit this one out. We have had enough adventures to last a lifetime for me, and I would love to stay here and help Talia get the new people here situated and maybe even set up my area in my…or, I mean, *our* room." She looked at Talia and smiled.

"Sounds good, Audrey," I said. I couldn't help but smile at her. Her smile was contagious, and I was happy she liked it here so much. "Bucket can stay here with you and keep you company. I also think we need to wear some nicer clothes, maybe a button-up or a nice polo, so we won't stand out so much when we walk in the door. What do you think?"

"I'm in," said Carl.

"You know I can't let you drive yourselves," added Sam.

"You guys going to just stand around all day, or are you actually doing something for a change?" a voice yelled from the front of the gym, where Nate stood next to Joe holding more boxes.

Sam jumped down off the stage and walked toward his brother. "You know I can carry twice as much as you, so I have the luxury of taking my time when I want!" Sam said, as he laughed and ran past Nate back toward the truck.

"Talia!" Joe yelled out. "Good to see you again. How is everything coming along?"

"Great!" Talia replied. "This is a good group to work with. They have been extremely helpful! We already have so much set up through the school, and everything on the stage is sorted and logged. Sam's checklist is making it easy on us, for sure."

"Well, I am about to ruin everything, then," Joe said. "I went to grab a generator from Scott's house, and I grabbed a bunch of other stuff while I was there, including this awesome drone." He grabbed the drone from the box he was carrying and lifted it into the air.

"Oh, I could have some fun with that!" Owen exclaimed.

"I'm sure we can go through the stuff pretty quickly. We have a lot of hands. Just keep bringing them all to me," Talia said as she pushed more totes to the left side of the stage.

"Is there anything you think we may be short on?" Joe asked.

Talia looked down at her clipboard then back up at Joe. "We could probably use some more seed because part of me thinks we will be farming that field out back for an entire community."

"True," Joe replied. "Even people who don't live here and have not accepted Christ yet might still have refused the mark, so we may be feeding more than just the mouths here. I will do what I can to help everyone be fed physically and spiritually!

"Owen, I would like to put you in charge of security, if you are okay with that. We are going to need safe checkpoints and perimeter surveillance. Get some of those solar-powered cameras close to the road opening and a place where we can safely put our phones, OBUs, and any other devices that can be tracked in any way."

"I am way ahead of you on that, boss," Owen replied. "I have cameras set up at all the closest intersections to the school as well as at the entrance. I have a bunch of phones that I have connected to the satellites we are using. Those phones aren't directly connected to satellites, so we can only use them here on campus, but at least we will be able to communicate without the cell towers pinging anyone's phones here. I just got back from putting copper boxes a couple miles from the entrances. Since it's a conductive metal, it will block the phones from getting incoming or outgoing signals, so no one will be able to use them to track any of us. Anyone leaving the secured area should turn off their phones unless they need to use them or are in another safe location."

"Is all that necessary?" Carl asked, jumping off of the stage. "That makes it seem like people are currently after us to kill us or something."

"They may not be looking for us just yet," Joe replied, "but it is only a matter of time before we are considered a threat to national security for opposing the Global One leadership."

"Thinking of Sam as a threat to national security is hilarious!" Carl said, putting his fist up to his mouth as he laughed.

Sam was coming back toward the stage with another tote. He placed it, with a rather large drop, onto Carl's foot. Carl jumped back as if it had hurt, but we all knew he was pretending.

"Oh, I'm sorry," retorted Sam, "was that your foot? I mean, they are about two feet long, so they are kind of hard to miss."

Sam jumped back to avoid Carl's fist lunging toward his arm. They both laughed before realizing the rest of us were staring at them. They both jumped up straight at attention and looked at Talia, who was standing with her hands on her hips looking more and more like Mila by the moment.

"Sorry, Aunt Talia!" Sam said with haste, and he turned and ran toward the door to retrieve more boxes.

"Yeah, sorry, Miss T. I'll keep it in check," Carl said, following Sam to retrieve more items from the trucks.

Audrey and Talia put their arms down from their hips and faced each other as they simultaneously broke out into laughter. Audrey looked back up at Talia. "I think we are going to get along great!"

Chapter Twenty-One

After all the boxes had been unloaded and sorted, Joe had us all come down to the chapel together to pray and have group devotional time before dinner. He wanted to make another trip to Franklin to get items from Carl and Aniyah's house as well as Audrey's house. We had packed like we were going on vacation, not like we were never coming back to our homes.

I was excited about the group devotional. Joe said he would be going over parts of Revelation that we might be able to relate to. We all grabbed our Bibles and headed down to the chapel. I never would have pictured going from living by myself to living with a bunch of people, some of whom I didn't know, and like it, but I surprisingly loved it. The camaraderie felt different from when I'd been amongst groups of people at school.

Joe said we were going to go over the seven seals. I couldn't recall ever learning about this in Sunday school, so when he started listing White Horse, Red Horse, Black Horse, and Pale Horse, I thought it sounded like a Dr. Seuss book. But then he listed the fifth seal as souls crying out from under the altar, and my thoughts of childhood nursery rhymes came to a quick halt.

Joe began to read Revelation 5:9: "'And they sang a new song, saying: "You are worthy to take the scroll and open its seals, because you were slain, and with your blood you purchased for God persons from every tribe and language and people and nation."'"

I looked up, ready to hear more. I glanced over at Carl, whose gaze was fixated on his Bible. Joe continued, "My grandfather told me when I was younger that people used to use seals in legal documents. Seals could be made with wax or even clay imprinted with a stamp. Different sections of the documents would be sealed, and many times the seals would be opened by a judge. The seals would keep the integrity and validity of the documents. Here, Jesus is the Lamb and rightful heir of this world, so only He has authority here to open the seals. The seals are seven periods of time that start after the Rapture. It starts out with the four different-colored horses, and that is where we get the four horsemen of the apocalypse. We start out with peace just like we saw with the signing of the peace treaty just a few years ago. Unfortunately, after that, it is anything but peace. Jesus describes it in Matthew as birth pains, and if you ask Mila, she will tell you that things get worse and worse as well as closer and closer together when you are describing birth pains!"

Carl gulped. I looked over at Audrey, and she looked at me, took a deep breath, and looked back down at her Bible. We had been preparing for the worst, but the idea of getting through it was still inconceivable to me.

"The good news is that these birth pains all lead to the coming of Christ. We know we have this to look forward to, and we know everything is temporary. We will lose people during this time, but we know that we will see them again soon. The souls mourning under the altar show how we will be persecuted. It has already begun. Aniyah was arrested earlier this week. Praise God she is here with us tonight, but we aren't going to be getting off so easily in the near future. This is going to escalate rather quickly. This is why we are here now."

Joe closed his Bible. "I encourage you all to read through chapter six tonight. When you are done, reread it, and then discuss it with each other. Nate and I will be heading out after we eat, so if any of you have any questions, you can catch me before we head out. But I will be back tonight, and we can finish going over the seals more tomorrow after you have all read through this chapter."

Everyone started to get up and move around the room, but I wanted to read the rest of the chapter quickly before dinner started. After I finished chapter six, I went onto chapter seven and then went back to chapter five again. I was sure glad Joe could help us navigate through this.

While I was finishing chapter five, I heard Carl's aunt Aniyah call from the doorway to the chapel, "Everyone, you can all come over to the home-ec room. We made spaghetti and meatballs with a chunky vegetable sauce."

Carl seemed to jump five feet into the air as he launched from his seat. "You don't have to tell me twice!"

The food smelled amazing. I grabbed a huge plate and smothered it in parmesan cheese.

"I hope you enjoy it," Aniyah said. "We have enough stored dried pasta to feed armies for a couple years, so we may be eating this a lot."

"I have no objections," I replied. "It tastes amazing, thank you! I know this must have cost a lot of money, too."

"Food is very expensive, for sure," Aniyah replied. "But a lot of this came from food stores like the one your parents left for you. Other people had some food stores as well, and the Sterns had done a lot of canning and prep, too. We owe you a big thanks for helping provide so much food and supplies here."

"Oh, don't thank me. I had very little to do with it," I said. I walked away with my plate and thanked God for all His provisions. I had taken for granted all the food I'd had during the past few years when I had known so many in my school were struggling each day.

While I was praying, Joe began to pray out loud, thanking God for the food and His Son and for mercy through these next few years.

After dinner, we all went to our rooms, unpacked our stuff, and settled in. I placed the picture of my family on the side table next to the bottom bunk. Carl jumped onto the top bunk above mine. I could see his feet hanging off the end of the bed above me.

"Make sure you wash your dogs so I don't smell those things down here," I yelled.

"My feet always smell like sweet cherry blossoms," Carl said as he dangled his head from the bed to look at me.

"If that's the case, then I don't want to smell a cherry blossom because I have smelled your feet plenty, and it ain't good, bruh," I said as I snickered.

Within minutes, I could hear Carl snoring. Bucket looked at me as if there were a strange animal in the room. "Don't worry Bucket, it's just Carl." With that, Bucket laid his head back down, and I prayed for guidance for our day tomorrow then fell asleep.

I woke up Tuesday morning before the sun came out and noticed more of our personal items were in the room. Joe and Nate must have brought them in last night while I had slept. I went down to the locker rooms and took a shower. The water had an iron smell to it, and the shower floor was stained red from the rust. I threw on a white button-up shirt and black dress slacks and walked back toward the shared bedroom. Mila must have joined us some time last night, as she was already in the home-ec room making pancakes in large batches.

"Good morning," I said. "You and your sister look a lot alike."

"I will take that as a compliment," Mila replied. "She was always way more talented than I was in everything, though. She did sports in high school but was also good at the arts and got straight As. I was more of a homebody, but I think I'm a better cook." She winked at me then continued flipping pancakes.

I grabbed a few off of a plate and ate them with my hands as I headed back to the room. Carl and Sam both passed me with their towels as they headed to the locker room, and Carl gave me a whistle. "Looking sharp, my man!"

Audrey walked out of her room just in time to hear Carl, and she looked at me and smiled. "I must say, Mr. Killian, you do dress up well. I would even go as far as saying you look quite handsome."

I blushed, awkwardly smiled, and kept walking back to the room to put away my things. I felt a rumble under my feet. It was a small earthquake, a gentle reminder that just because we were in a new place did not mean we didn't have the same problems.

Owen came to the room and stood in the doorway.

"I'm ready when you guys are. You can grab me from the office when you are ready to head out. I have everything ready. I just need to grab my laptop and the key card."

"Sounds good, brother."

While I waited on Carl and Sam, I went to Audrey's room to tell her goodbye. Her door was open, and she and Talia were decorating the walls. It looked like they had been living there for a while already. Arranged on top of a big area rug in the center was a small couch, an assortment of pillows, and a bean bag chair. The walls were covered with twinkle lights and colorful pictures as well as handmade calendars and scripture verses. The desks already had knick-knacks, and the beds were covered with soft blankets, fluffy pillows, and a couple of stuffed animals. They had even utilized the dry-erase board with a daily scripture reading schedule on one side and a daily workout schedule on the other side as well as a list of chores and jobs to do around the school.

"Wow, you all work fast," I exclaimed. "This looks great. You may have to help us guys out when you are done. We still have plain cement white walls, and it looks like a prison cell compared to this."

The women laughed, and Audrey made her way over to me. "So are you guys getting ready to leave soon?"

"Yeah, I wanted to come over and say goodbye first," I replied. "We have been spending every minute of every day together lately that it almost feels weird that you aren't coming, but I'm glad you are able to make friends and help out around here, too."

"Yeah, I thought it would be good for me to get to know Talia better and help her out. She has had her hands full here getting everything ready for us."

"I also wanted to talk to you for a minute," I continued. "I think it's obvious that I have feelings for you, but I wanted to make sure I told you. I have no idea how this time will turn out for us, and I don't even know if there is a future for our relationship, but I think we should both pray about it. In the meantime, I will miss you." I bent down and kissed her on the cheek then wrapped my arms around her and gave her a big hug. For a moment, it felt like this was the last time I would see her.

"I care about you, too, silly boy," she said with her head buried in my chest.

Talia looked up at us and smiled. "You boys come back safe!"

"Sam does a pretty good job of taking care of us," I replied. "Take good care of Bucket while I'm gone."

"We will. I think he may have fun going out and checking on the goats with me," Talia replied.

As I headed back to our room, Carl and Sam came around the corner wearing button-up shirts and dress slacks.

"I don't know about you two, but I make this look good," Carl said, pinching down the collar of his shirt.

"Sure you do, Carl," Sam said as he ran past him to our room.

Audrey caught back up with me before I walked in the doorway. She held a folded piece of paper. "Here is a phone number that you can reach me at while I'm here. Once you get your phone, text me so I know you guys are still okay."

"I will." I hugged her one more time before Sam, Carl, and I headed out of the school to the car. Sam's mom had driven the car here the night before, so we were able to drive that instead of the truck again. Carl sat in the front, and I sat in the back with Owen.

"This entire town is pretty much deserted," Owen said as we drove along the pathway in the woods. "These precautions are mostly for satellite systems and technology security."

After we pulled onto the main road, we were able to grab our phones and put the on-board unit back on the car. "If we come across any trouble, I've been able to hack the OBU. They still won't be able to track us, they will just think they can," Owen said.

"Good to know," Sam said as he put the car into drive.

The drive seemed longer this time. We passed houses on which all the windows had been broken. I wondered if that would happen to my house soon. As we drove closer to Indianapolis, we started to see more people, and along with the people, we saw more trash, graffiti, and broken homes. The tents up along the highway outnumbered the houses in the town we were staying in. Small smoke stacks were scattered among the tents from the fires people had made to keep warm. Even in June, the mornings were cool and damp, and the smog made the city seem that much colder.

"I haven't been to Indianapolis in years. I didn't know things had gotten this bad," I exclaimed. The once-thriving city looked like nothing more than a large homeless camp.

"The sad thing is that a lot of these people are picked up by the authorities and taken to the social security building to get registered and set up with the chip with promises of food. Then once they get it, they are dropped back off here with empty bellies," Owen said.

The roads hadn't been taken care of, and we were dodging potholes every few seconds. There weren't very many vehicles on the road. We passed a few buses and semi-trailers but saw very few cars.

We parked a couple blocks down from my dad's office. The amount of facial recognition screens and advertisement boards were endless in this area. I couldn't walk two steps before hearing another ad. My dad's office building had dark, sleek architectural features that were alluring but not very inviting and a large sign that stood out from the rest. The sign said, KILLIAN TECH INNOVATIONS.

Chapter Twenty-Two

My heart skipped a beat as I looked up at the sign. Every time I had been here as a child, I had felt excited, but this time I felt quite different. I felt a blast from my past mixed with nostalgia, a longing for what I had once had alongside a determination to never go back.

Owen instructed us to walk in like we owned the place. We had to walk past reception to reach the elevator that would take us to the fourteenth floor, which housed my dad's old office.

We walked past the reception desk without making eye contact, but the receptionist did a double take as I walked by as if she had recognized me.

"Good morning," I said.

"Good morning," she replied, sounding a bit puzzled. She didn't stop us or call anyone, so we headed toward the elevator.

The office floor directory noted the two offices on the fourteenth floor belonged to Doug Killian and Genevieve Barts. I wanted to know who this Barts lady was and if she was the one behind some of the crooked stuff my dad's company—and Max—were into.

We stepped in, and I pulled out the key card. I scanned it and was prompted to place my thumbprint on the pad below. I looked at Owen but placed my thumb on the pad before he had a chance to respond, and it turned green. I hit the number fourteen, and the elevator began to rise.

"That was not me," Owen said, slightly confused and caught off guard. "I looked into this place, and nothing I saw led me to believe they had a multi-factor authentication with biometrics."

"I remember using my thumb last time I was here, and it worked in the elevator. I thought it was so cool. My dad let me use my thumb every time. I guess I'm still in the system," I said, reassuring Owen.

One by one, the floors came and went until we arrived on floor nine. The elevator stopped, and a tall blonde woman stepped onto it. She was well dressed, and her mark was predominately placed in the center of her forehead. All four of us instinctively put our hands behind our backs as if we naturally stood that way, but in reality, we were hiding the lack of a mark on our own hands.

She looked at me out of the corner of her eye then looked forward then back to me. "I'm sorry, have we met? You don't look familiar, and I've been working here for over two years."

"I work on a research team, so most of my work is out of town. I'm just here today for a brief, uh, inspection, so to speak, and then heading back out of town this afternoon. Glad you've been with us a couple years, you must like it," I said before glancing at Sam and Carl. Both of them looked at me with their eyes wide open.

"Oh, yes, I do. Thank you. You look so young to sound so important," she said as the doors opened up on the eleventh floor. She looked at the lit-up fourteenth button and looked back at me. "Fourteenth floor, huh? Well, you must be important. The name's Rita. You can look me up anytime." She stepped out of the elevator and turned left as the doors shut.

"Okay, that was the smoothest talking I have ever seen you do," Carl said as he put both his hands on my shoulder.

"Well, this is the best research team I have ever worked with," I said as I laughed.

The elevator chime went off as the doors opened on the fourteenth floor. Across from the elevator was a semi-opaque wall in front of which water was coming down into a rock bed. *KTI, Paving the Way to a Better Global Community* was written across the front. To the right was the secretary's office and a boardroom, and to the left was my dad's old office right next to Genevieve Barts's office.

We could hear voices coming from the secretary's office, so we quickly made our way to my dad's office and scanned the key card. I pressed my thumb to the pad, and the door made a clicking sound and opened as I pulled it.

We all rushed into the office and shut the door behind us. Owen went straight to the computer on the desk. Sam started going through files adjacent to Owen, and Carl and I walked around the room. The office was almost exactly as I remembered it. My kindergarten picture was still placed on the shelf next to some books.

Carl bent down, opened the mini fridge, and pulled out two cans of Coke. "Want one?" He extended a can toward me.

"I mean, yeah, but isn't that stealing?" I asked back.

"Well, technically, this is still your dad's office, and I'm pretty sure he would think it was okay," Carl replied as he popped the top to his can of Coke.

I shrugged and said, "Okay, hand it over."

"This is interesting," Owen said after a few moments on the computer. "Since you never reported your parents missing, this company is still operated with him as the primary stockholder."

"What does that mean, exactly?" I asked.

"Well, he has it set up that if he dies, those stocks go directly to you. In essence, if you claimed that he disappeared, you would be running this company instead of that Barts lady. She must have realized that he disappeared and knew you didn't report it. She must have taken over with your dad's name still in charge. The money that your dad was making was still being directly deposited into your account this entire time, but someone must have tried to get access to those funds without raising too many suspicious flags, so they had the money being transferred into Max's account slowly over time. Max's name is even on a file on this laptop with a list of jobs."

"You've got to be kidding me." I started pacing. "All this time? He has been working for my dad's company? Doing what, exactly? Just spying on me?"

Sam bent down and looked at Max's info on the computer. "Sorry to say this, man, but it looks like he was hired before we ever met him. It looks like he was recruited to befriend you and keep you close and to try and sway you to make certain decisions."

The office door opened, and Max stood in the doorway, giving Sam a slow clap. "Well, the genius has finally figured it out."

"Max? How could you?" I was desperate to find closure for the loss of my friend standing right in front of me.

"I was the right age and lived in the right area. Basically, I got lucky. A guy approached me one day and said he would give me a job and pay me fairly well, and all I had to do was go about my everyday life and pal around with you. Of course, if there was anything new that ever came up, I had to report that, so when you found that letter, I let him know right away." Max seemed both arrogant and confident, very different from the Max I thought I had known over the years.

"So you were never my friend?" I asked, as I took a step closer and looked directly into his eyes.

"Quite the contrary, Scott, I was probably your best friend and still am, unlike these guys who keep dragging you into a life of poverty and crime."

I chuckled at the audacity. "How do you figure that?"

"Scott, don't you know what you have here?" Max asked with complete sincerity. "This company is worth millions in the Babylonian exchange, if not billions! This is a company that is changing the world over. You have the power to do whatever you want. To buy whatever you want. To create whatever you want. All you have to do is accept it."

"I thought you were trying to prevent me from taking over the company. Weren't you hired so I would keep my mouth shut about my father disappearing so that whoever hired you could control the company instead of me?"

"Oh, Scott, you have it all wrong!"

Owen closed the laptop and looked at me. He motioned to the door with his head then looked at Carl and Sam and repeated the gesture. As Owen, Carl, and Sam started to inch their way to the door, I tried to buy time with Max.

"Okay, so tell me then, what is your great plan? To have me run this company?"

"There is no great scheme, Scott, you just come in here and do it. Legally, this company is yours. Just come in here and run the place."

"So just like that, huh?" I asked, making sure Max was making direct eye contact with me so everyone else could leave the room. Then I realized I not only had the key card, but my friends might also need my thumbprint to get off of the fourteenth floor. I started to step sideways, keeping Max in front of me so I could make my way to the door.

"Well, in order to be completely legal, you would still have to get the mark, but it's just a chip in your hand. It's no different than the key card you used in the elevator, only implanted so no one else can use it. It's not as big of a deal as you are making it out to be. You just don't want to comply with any authority."

"I mean, I would have to pledge my allegiance and devotion to Gabby Gabe to get it, too."

"Just lie. It's not like they are going to hook you up to a lie detector test to know if you really worship the guy or not. You are making your life harder for yourself when you don't have to." Max sounded irritated.

I was finally in a position to run to the door and beat Max out. I didn't have a plan, and I wasn't sure of the lengths to which Max would go to stop me, either. I counted in my head to three and ran toward the door, slamming it shut behind me. The other three were already on the elevator and holding the door open. I tapped my key card and hit the button for floor one with my thumb. The door to the elevator closed as soon as we saw Max approach. The elevator seemed to take an eternity to descend, and before it could make it to the first floor, it came to a complete halt, and the lights went out.

"Come on, help me pry this door open!" I cried out.

We dug our fingers between the doors and opened them to reveal that we were halfway below the eleventh floor. We pulled ourselves up and out of the elevator.

"Come on this way!" Owen said as he took off to the right. He had studied the floor plans for the building, so I guessed he remembered where we could find another exit.

None of the people working at their desks looked up, which made me believe a high security threat hadn't been activated yet. Off in the distance, I could see a security officer grab his walkie, but I couldn't make out what was being said to him.

As we kept walking, I noticed the blonde lady from the elevator at one of the desks. "Rita! I'm glad to see a familiar face. Look, someone has broken into my dad's office upstairs. I think they may be trying to escape. Can you call security and have a team of them go up to the twelfth floor? And tell them to hurry!"

"Oh my, yes! I will call them right away!" After Rita called security, the guard in the corner listened to his walkie again then ran to the stairwell.

We ran to the stairwell and down the stairs, hearing the security guard's footsteps heading up the stairs above us. At the seventh floor, the door started to open. Sam and Owen were already past the stairwell entrance, but Carl and I were still on the stairs right above the door.

"Keep going!" I whispered to Sam and Owen. Carl and I both turned around, went up to the eighth-floor stairwell door, and ran through it. The floor plan was vastly different from that of the eleventh floor.

"Where are we?" Carl whispered, hunched close to my ear.

"It looks like this is the projects floor. I remember my dad talking about all the new things they were working on. He would bring me here to show me the latest gadget or robot. They have different rooms set up like labs where different teams work on their projects. I don't see too many people working right now."

The lights in the hallway were dark, leading us to assume the teams had gone to lunch. As we waited to see if the stairwell was clear, we heard more steps coming up.

"Come on," I said, "there is an outside balcony where the team takes cigarette breaks and lunches. There is an outside stairwell we can access from the balcony."

"You know I hate heights. You already had me climb out of the window of your house, and that was bad enough, but now we are eight stories high," Carl half-whispered, half-yelled.

"It's not that bad, I promise. I used those stairs before when I was a kid, and if it was safe enough for my mom, then trust me, it's fine. I'll text Sam and tell him which way we are going and to meet us near the car."

I pulled out my phone, and the piece of paper with Audrey's phone number fell out of my pocket onto the floor. I sighed and picked it up. Audrey had told me to text her that we were safe. We weren't, but if something happened to us, I didn't want her to never hear from us again, so I unfolded the paper and punched the number into my phone. I didn't know what to say, as I didn't want to lie, so I texted the words, *I love you*, then quickly texted Sam the plan.

After a second, Sam texted back, *Okay*, so Carl and I ran toward the back of the building. There were a few stragglers out on the balcony, but they were all too preoccupied on their phones to give Carl or me a second look.

"Over here!" I said, pointing to the outside staircase. In front of the entrance to the stairs was a gate. "Ugh. It's locked. We can just climb over. It shouldn't be that hard." I jumped on top of the gate and had to slide my stomach over a little before I could swing my legs over to the other side. It was a little harder than I had thought it would be, but I made it across.

I looked down to the bottom of the stairs and didn't see anyone coming. "Looks clear this way. I think we may be able to go all the way to the bottom without having to go back inside the building. There does look like there may be another gate at the bottom, though."

"The quicker we get out of here, the better," Carl said as he jumped up and pulled himself onto the gate. The moment he started to slide his stomach over and pull his legs around, the entire building started to shake. The earthquake made Carl lose his balance, and he slid too far. His legs dropped below him, and he hung on to the side of the building. For a moment, I thought Carl had fallen eight stories down to the ground.

I jumped up on the rail and reached my hand down. Carl's hand slipped from the rail and grabbed onto the ledge below. I threw myself over the rail, holding on with one hand and reaching down to help Carl with my other hand.

"Hang on there, Carl! I got you!"

The fear in Carl's face hurt me deeply. He looked down and then back up at me, sweat pouring from his head and hands, which kept slipping from my grasp whenever I tried to grab them.

"I can't hold on!" Carl yelled out.

"Don't say that! I just need to get a better grip of your hand!"

Carl looked me in the eyes. The fear on his face had melted away. A look of peace had come over him.

"It's okay!" he said.

Tears filled my eyes. "Carl, I love you, man, you're my best friend. I'm not ready to let go yet."

"Take good care of Sam, he needs it."

Tears were pouring down my cheeks. Carl's hands were slipping more and more, and I couldn't hold on any longer. With the last strength that I had, I tried one more time to pull him up, and as his hand slipped through mine, another hand from behind me reached down and grabbed onto Carl's wrist. With the other person's help, I was able to grab onto Carl's other wrist and pull him up far enough so that Carl could use his feet to push himself up further and we could pull him up over the rail.

I grabbed onto Carl and drew him into my chest with such force that I knocked the wind out of him. Carl caught his breath and hugged me back.

"Good thing you didn't lose me! You probably wouldn't last long without me," Carl joked.

"Shut up, you!" I said and hugged him even tighter.

A moment later, it dawned on me that I had had help pulling up Carl. I turned around to thank the man.

"Dad?"

Chapter Twenty-Three

My dad stood before me like a mirage in a desert. It was hard for me to believe what my eyes were seeing. Was I dreaming? A large group of security guards came running onto the balcony.

"Arrest them!" my dad said. His long dark coat looked all too familiar, though he didn't have on the blue Colts hat.

I looked to Carl for confirmation that I was seeing whom I thought I was seeing. Carl looked at me and shook his head, clearly not knowing what to say.

"DAD!" I cried out.

Max walked onto the balcony with a middle-aged, dark-haired woman. The guards placed handcuffs on me and Carl.

"Where are your other two friends?" my dad asked as the woman came up and put her arm around him.

I stared at him in disbelief.

"Scott! Where are your friends?" he asked again. This time, his voice was raised and a familiar tone of exasperation and disappointment.

"I'm sure they are long gone by now," I said, hoping my words were true. I knew Sam wouldn't leave without me or Carl, but I was fairly certain Owen would have been able to sense trouble and taken everyone to a more secure location while keeping an eye on our rendezvous point. "Who is your friend?"

The woman took her arm off my dad. "Genevieve Barts. Your dad has told me so much about you." She motioned to the guards.

"Take these two down to the station and have them hold them," my dad told the guards. Without so much as a glance my way, he brushed by me to return to the building with Barts. "Let them know I'll be down later to handle it."

"I told you you should have joined me, Scott," Max said snidely as the guards started walking Carl and I to the door.

"So my dad is the one that hired you to pretend to be my friend?"

Max shrugged and laughed. "He even paid me straight from his account that you were using, but you were too dumb to notice."

I lunged toward Max. The guards held me back, but I pulled closer to him and said, "I loved you like a brother."

Max's smile faded, and he turned away from us and went back inside the building. The guards quickly followed, dragging us along. We were put into the elevator and brought down to the first floor. I looked around for any sign of Sam or Owen but didn't see anything suspicious. On the way out, I smiled at the receptionist, who put her head down as if embarrassed we had walked right by her earlier.

The guards put Carl and me in the back of a police car. The officer behind the wheel was stocky with a dark mustache and didn't say a word the entire time we were with him. We drove by where we had originally parked, but there was no sign of Sam's car. I sighed in relief and nodded to the spot while looking at Carl. He nodded back and smiled. We were sure our friends had gotten away.

I felt my phone going off in my pocket, but I couldn't reach it. I slid myself over and butted up the phone to Carl's hands. He pulled the phone out and dropped it on the seat next to us. I looked down and saw a text from Sam.

"*Saw blue and red. Returning. Ditch phone*," I whispered to Carl. "They must have seen us get arrested, so they went back. I'm not sure how we can ditch the phone before we go into the precinct, though."

Just then, the car stopped in front of a two-story concrete building, out front of which were a couple of trees and shrubs. I decided I would hold my phone behind my back until we were closer to the shrub then pretend to sneeze and drop it. If it worked, great, and if it didn't, then I would be no worse off than if I hadn't tried at all.

The officer that had been driving escorted Carl and me to the front entrance. As soon as we passed the shrub, I gave my fake sneeze and tossed my phone as hard as I could.

The officer tightened his grip on my arm and said, "Move it."

Inside the station, we were patted down. The officer took Carl's phone and my gum wrapper from the stick of gum Owen had offered me.

"This all you got on you?" the officer asked me.

"I try to keep a low profile," I replied.

The officer wasn't amused and walked us back to a cell. It was a few feet deep and longer than it was deep. It had a bench on both walls and another in the middle, and the walls were an ugly dull orange color. Carl sat down on a bench and looked like he was deep in thought.

"You okay, man?" I asked.

"To be honest, yeah. Surprisingly good," Carl said as he looked up at me and smiled. "I have never been arrested before, and for the first time in my life, I don't think my aunt will be mad at me for it!"

I laughed a little along with Carl, but my laugh sounded more awkward and nervous than authentic.

"I know earlier must have been hard on you, too," I said despite my reluctance to bring up Carl's near-death experience.

Carl put his hand on my shoulder. "You know what, I'm okay with that, too." He dropped his hand and continued. "All my life I've been scared. Scared of failure, scared of death, scared of life, even, but at that moment, I prayed for help. It wasn't the help that made me feel different. It was the peace I felt after I prayed. I just felt that no matter what happens, God is in control. I'm either going to go on helping you and doing His work here, or I'm going to be with Him in heaven, and I'm good either way." Carl smiled, and I could see the peace come over him just as I had seen earlier. "Now, about that new elephant in the room. So, like, are we going to talk about how your dad is a supervillain trying to take over the world or…yeah?"

"Heh, yeah, that, uh, was definitely unexpected," I said with my hands together and my head tilted down. "You know, the funny thing was that I never remembered my dad being saved. I knew without a doubt my mom was, but she always seemed to be witnessing to my dad and me both, and he didn't seem to have time for it, or for her, for that matter. I thought I must have missed something when Joe started talking about the Rapture."

"And now he has us locked up," Carl snickered. "Well, for what it's worth, I'm glad I'm the one stuck in here with you, and I'm glad we are having this adventure together. No matter what happens from here, I know I'll see you again someday, and I know where I'm going."

Carl's words struck me. The goofy frightful boy I had known since the playground at Creekside Elementary School was sitting next to me now as a man that I looked up to.

"So do you have any Bible verses memorized?" Carl asked.

"Maybe just a few. My mom had me memorize some when I was younger in Sunday School. Why do you ask?"

"We may be stuck in here a long time, and I highly doubt that a Bible will be eligible to be put on our reading list. I was kind of hoping you had some memorized to share with me."

"I do remember the one my mom quoted to me all the time. I would come in from playing outside and would be mad at Brian Wells for taking my cars or pushing me in the mud. My mom would say, 'Be kind to one another, tenderhearted, forgiving one another, even as God in Christ forgave you.' I remember it was in a book called Ephesians. It didn't mean much to me then, but it sure does mean a lot now."

"You are going to have to repeat that one to me a few times. I would love to memorize as many as I can," Carl said. His newfound love for God was encouraging.

After going over the verse together a few times, Carl seemed to have it memorized. He laid his head back on the metal bench, closed his eyes, and repeated the verse over and over until he fell asleep.

The minutes turned into hours. My stomach kept making gurgling sounds, and I tried to sleep to pass the time, but my body seemed to be rebelling against me for its lack of food. When a guard walked past at one point, I asked him if they would bring us anything to eat.

"Ha, yeah, right, punk. You'd be lucky if we gave you some water. What do you think this is? A vacation? If we provided meals in jail, half the population would be committing crimes just to get in here to get a plate of food. I barely make enough here at this job to buy food for myself and my family. If they did give us food to give you guys, I would take it for myself and bring it home to my kids!"

Carl woke up in time to hear what the guard had said. "Guess it's a good thing I ate about twelve pancakes this morning before we left!"

I stood up, walked across the cell, and sat back down on the other side to keep my body from feeling so stiff. The door the guard had walked through opened again, and in walked my dad with another guard.

"Bring him to me in the back office. I need to have a word with him," my dad said, pointing to me.

The guard had me put my hands through the bars so he could handcuff me before letting me out. He directed me to a room that looked more like an interrogation room than it did an office.

My dad came into the room with a bag, the contents of which smelled like the meatloaf he used to make for me when I was younger. He placed the bag in front of me and took the handcuffs off me. "Here, eat."

"What about Carl?" I asked.

"Carl isn't my son. He isn't my concern."

"I didn't know that disappearing from my life for over three years is what 'concern' looked like," I said, making quotation marks with my fingers around the word *concern*.

"I hired Max to look out for you."

"You mean to spy on me," I retorted.

"I didn't want your mother swaying you to believe some nonsense that could cost you your life. Max was to help steer you away from all of that. Unfortunately, he failed, and I will most likely fire him."

"That must have been why he was so persistent about me coming to join the company. He wasn't concerned about me, he just didn't want to get fired. Nice. So why bother disappearing? Why couldn't you do the job yourself, you know, the job of being my dad and raising me?" I knew my anger and sarcasm were coming out, and I tried to think about how I should respond better in Christ rather than in anger.

"When your mom took off, I knew that she had found some things at the office, and she came to her own conclusion about them. I also knew that she wouldn't just abandon you, so I thought if it looked like I disappeared as well, she would eventually come back for you and bring you with her. Since I had Max keeping an eye on you, the minute she turned up, I would be able to recover the files and save my company.

"I paid Steven Whittaker from the office a thousand dollars to call you to see what you would tell him. When you told him I was traveling for business, disappearing just made sense, and no one would question anything. You never even called him back. I wanted to be close to you, Scott. It's not my fault you didn't recognize your own dad. Plus, I never figured that your mom would hide the files for you to find and not come back for you herself." My dad was pacing back and forth by the door as he spoke.

"First off, she didn't take off and abandon me. Only you did that. The fact that your company is more important to you than I am doesn't surprise me, though," I said, as I pushed the food back toward his side of the table. "Am I supposed to recognize you from a distance and assume that you didn't want to be close to me? I hardly recognize you now! The dad I knew wouldn't be dating some lady from his office while married to Mom. I just don't get you. If you hired Max to spy on me, why not just hire some more goons to chase me or do your dirty work for you?"

"I loved your mom. She was a handful, though. Some of that information your mother manipulated was important enough to me to hide from as many people as possible. By the time Max texted me from your room that night you found your mom's letter, there wasn't much time for me to get other people involved. I even planned on letting you see me that night. I hoped you would believe I had been incapacitated. The same thing happened the day you found something in the shed. Max was at work, and I tried to stop you before the damage was done, but you just had to make that video anyway. I hope you know you have put a lot of lives in jeopardy with that crap, son."

I had missed my parents so much over the years, and now my dad was standing in front of me, and I didn't even want to talk to him anymore. I felt that I had never known him to begin with. I looked down at the bag of food, which no longer looked desirable in any way. I felt a heaviness in my chest, and my face felt hot. I turned away from the food to the floor, where a beetle was slowly walking.

"Not hungry?" he asked.

"I just can't be bought," I replied.

"You think you are tough because you can refuse food after not eating for, what, less than a day? Maybe you'll change your tune after you haven't eaten for a couple of days." My dad walked to the door, opened it, and spoke to the guard standing on the other side, "Take him to his own cell."

The guard came in and replaced the handcuffs on my wrists. This time, he squeezed them so tightly I thought my wrists would bleed. He led me down a dark hallway and put me in a jail cell with one cot and one toilet. Both were filthy and smelled like mildew and urine. I sat down on my cot and began to pray.

I didn't know how long I was in the cell. The days blended into the nights, there were no windows, and no one came to bring me meals. There was a bucket of water in my cell that I occasionally reached into to drink from. I didn't see Carl or any other prisoner; I didn't see my dad. My prayers varied from asking for forgiveness for random things I remembered to thanking God for all His provisions throughout the last few years. There were even times I told Him jokes or talked to Him about the mice I saw crawling around my cell. I prayed for Carl, Sam, and Audrey.

The hunger I'd initially felt faded. The lack of food hurt my sense of balance more than it hurt my stomach. I wasn't sure if I would ever see anyone again or if I would die in this cell, but just as I noticed I had run out of water, a guard came by and brought me another bucket. I knew they were watching me. I knew my dad was waiting for me to give up.

"Lord, please be my strength!" I shouted.

Shortly afterward, the door to the cell opened.

Chapter Twenty-Four

A guard stood in the doorway of my cell. It was evident he was not bringing me water as his hands were empty. "Stand up. You're coming with me."

I was unable to stand. My brain was telling my legs to move, but I didn't have the power to move them.

"I said stand up," he said as he came into the cell. He grabbed me off the cot and pulled me to my feet. "Let's go." He pushed me out of the cell door and into the hallway.

My feet managed to stumble before me and keep me upright as I faltered down the hall. The guard led me to the same room I had been in the last time I'd seen my dad. Moments after the door shut, my dad walked back into the room with another bag of food and put it in front of me.

"Eat!" he demanded.

I didn't move. I didn't speak. My dad grabbed the bag, pulled out a sandwich, opened the wrapper to reveal a large cheeseburger, and set it in front of me.

"Eat it," he said again, frustration building in his voice. "You've been in that cell for nine days."

I stared at it for a minute then turned my head to stare at the corner of the room.

"So you're just going to starve to death to prove how much you hate me?" he asked.

I looked up at him and mustered the energy to talk. "I don't hate you. I love you. You're my dad. But I do feel like you hate me. I would never lock you in a cell and starve you just to prove a point."

The frustration left my dad's face. He placed his hands on his hips, turned his back to me, and faced the other side of the room. "Scott, you are my son, and I love you, but you are right, I needed to make a point. If you continue believing in your God and defying your true leader, it will only lead you to starvation and death. I had to show you the path that you are choosing. You can't keep going on with your delusions!"

"Dad, at this point, I'm okay with dying. I'm not scared of what death will bring me. I am scared of what death will bring you. I know you have made your decision, and for whatever reason, you decided to reject God, but I won't. I made mistakes before by not listening to Mom, but I won't make that mistake again. I can't get the mark. I can never join your company and this agenda to rid Christians. I *will* tell people to refuse the mark."

My dad sat down across from me and sighed.

"Where is Carl?" I asked. I presumed he had been in a cell like mine, starving and not knowing if he would ever see me again on this earth.

I couldn't tell if my dad looked angry or as if he was going to cry. "He's gone," he said sternly.

"What do you mean by *gone*?" I asked, unsure if I was prepared for the answer.

"We gave him several opportunities to tell us where you guys were hiding out and several opportunities to get the mark and pledge his allegiance to Friedman, and he refused. It was his choice."

"What was his choice?" I asked. I had a lump in my throat, but I didn't tear up. I wanted my dad to know I was ready to make the same choice as Carl. That I could be strong, too, and that my faith in Christ was unwavering.

"He was killed yesterday," my dad said emotionlessly. He had known Carl since Carl had been a little boy yet seemed as though he was talking about a murderer on death row.

The lump in my throat grew. I wanted to cry out, to scream at my dad, to curse him out loud, but I closed my eyes and prayed silently in my head instead. I stayed quiet until my dad started talking again.

"I just don't understand why neither of you will take the mark. It's a free gift. You can have access to anything you need, you won't go to jail, you won't be killed, and you can live comfortably. All you have to do is accept it."

"Oddly enough, Dad, salvation is a free gift, too. The biggest difference is that I would be giving up eternity in exchange for mere convenience with the gift you are offering." Tears formed in my eyes. I wasn't sure if they were for the loss of Carl or the eternal loss of my dad or both. "You love your money so much that you will sacrifice everything else, your wife, your son, your eternity, just so you can hold onto it for a short while longer. It is only a matter of time before things start to get worse, and your money will be worthless, anyway."

"You're going to suffer for your faith," he said.

"Yeah, apparently at the hands of my own dad." I stared him directly in the eyes. He couldn't dispute that he was responsible for all the suffering I had gone through. "What did you do to Gary?"

"I don't know any Gary," he muttered.

"I guess I shouldn't expect you to know people's names. He was the bus driver that couldn't even remember who I was. He was a friend of mine, too."

"Oh, the bus driver. He broke the rules. I gave him a choice. He let me do an experiment on him with the promise of getting him his job back. Everyone has a choice, son."

"Did you kill Russell, too? Did he have a choice?"

"I did what I had to do to try to stop you from spreading confidential information about the company. He had the choice not to break the law. I tried to stop you before that, but you just had to keep going. I have sacrificed a lot to get you here so that you could have an easy life, Scott."

"Sacrificed a lot? You mean like Carl, Gary, and Russell? I'm not a little kid anymore that will believe every narcissistic thing you have to say. Blame everyone but yourself, but this is your doing, Dad. You're not going to gaslight me into thinking this is anyone's fault but yours. You have no one to blame but yourself, and I forgive you."

He stared at me with glazed-over eyes. Forgiveness was the one thing that was not offered by the Antichrist. His regime was anything but forgiving, and I could sense my dad understood that. He turned away from me, stared at the door for a few minutes, then walked out of the room. He looked back over his shoulder once then disappeared down the hallway. The door remained open, and my handcuffs were not put back on.

I stood up, grabbed the food, and walked out the door. No guard was standing by. I made my way to the front of the building and walked out the front door. I finally saw a guard walking back to the front desk, but he didn't look up or see me. I walked down the steps, reached down to the shrubs, and retrieved my phone. It was dead.

I consumed the burger with a savageness I was not used to, and it almost made me sick. As I walked down the sidewalk, hiccups started coming so strong and frequently they hurt my body. I thought I could remember the way back to the shelter if I took the same route that had brought me here, but I didn't have a vehicle, and it had been over an hour away by car.

I had only walked for about thirty minutes before the dizziness and fatigue started to take over. After not having eaten for nine days, I didn't know how much farther I could go before collapsing. I stuck out my thumb, and several cars passed by. The noise of the cars and the sunlight were enough to make my head spin, and nausea came over me. Just as my vision started darkening, I heard a car pull over. It was a beat-up, spray-painted car with piles of stuff in the back seat. The window was down, and I bent over to look in the car.

In the driver's seat sat an older man with a full beard and gray scattered throughout his hair. "Need a ride, man?"

I sat in the front seat of his car and closed my eyes for a moment.

"Hey, man, you don't look so good. Where ya headed?"

"About an hour east on this road," I managed to say.

He looked at me carefully. "Looks like you don't have the mark. Any other way you could pay me for the ride?"

I looked back at him and noticed he didn't have the mark either. "All I have is this phone. It works if you plug it in. It's yours if you want it." I figured since it wasn't charged it would be no good to me until I arrived at the shelter, and by then, I wouldn't need it.

"I'm more interested in food, but it doesn't look like you've been eating much. I'll take you as far as I can. Should be pretty close to where you are going."

"Are you a Christian?" I asked.

"No, I'm just not a fan of being forced to give up who I am just so someone can tell me what I can and can't buy or what I can and can't do."

I didn't want to invite him to the shelter if it would compromise the others, but I figured I had an hour to talk to the man on the way. "I put out a video about the chip not that long ago. It shows the dangers of—"

"That was you?" he asked with excitement. "Oh, I've seen that video. I admire you, man. That took some gumption! The name's Nick, by the way."

"Scott." I smiled knowing that my video had had an impact on a complete stranger. I continued to talk about the Bible, the Rapture, the Antichrist, and salvation through Christ that God gave to us. It was my first time sharing the Gospel with someone.

"Up there on the right is where I need to go." I pointed up ahead. "You know, you can come with me if you want. We have some food and supplies saved up, and we have Bible studies and a church service every Sunday."

"Man, I have to tell ya, been wantin' to learn more about your God. Been kinda lost for a while now, just trying to find a way." He pulled over to the side of the road as I instructed, and we got out of the car to leave my phone and his car's on-board unit. We stepped back into the car, and he started to tear up. We prayed together, and when we finished, the joy on his face was contagious. Had I not been arrested, I would have never met this man and led him to Jesus.

We jumped back out and moved the branches from the path. I stayed out of the car as he drove through the clearing then rejoined him in the car after pushing the branches back in front of the path. I was still weak but felt a resurgence of energy from praying with Nick and knowing I would see the rest of my friends soon, though I wasn't ready to tell them about Carl. I knew Aniyah's heart would be broken, but she would be proud to know that he had left this earth with great peace over him.

We pulled up to the gymnasium doors, which were propped open. We walked in to see dozens of people scattered around on cots throughout the gym. Most of them looked sick or hungry. I stood in the doorway and looked around the room.

Talia and Aniyah were carrying baskets of food and dividing the food among the people. Sam was helping a man limp across the floor toward a cot. Audrey was wrapping gauze around a young woman's leg. It looked like the same woman I had given food to at the Walmart just a few days before I had been arrested. I had missed a lot in the short time that I had been gone.

No one had seen me yet, though I was sure Owen had spotted us on the security cameras. I motioned for Nick to go talk to Sam about where to set himself up but stayed back myself. I wanted to look around and soak this all in.

I had left my dad behind for the final time, in my past. I looked at each face as I scanned the room and understood that this was my family. Sam looked toward me as he was talking to Nick. The joy on his face was indescribable. I saw Audrey rise to her feet with tears in her eyes. She started to run toward me.

This moment, this kinship, this family, is only the beginning. It is the precursor to the greatest fellowship, the greatest family, and the greatest reunion that will ever come. When Christ returns to reunite us with Him. The bride and the Bridegroom.

Epilogue

The room was cool and dark. There was water on the floor that had leaked through the opening that had once been a window. The toilet flushed, filling with the only water in the room to drink from. The petrichor emanating from the ground was a refreshing change from the smell of decaying flesh permeating the air from the many rodents that infested the cell block.

The only sounds that could be heard were an occasional siren and chimes from a nearby clock. The striking of the clock was the only way for prisoners to keep their sanity in the dark and otherwise timeless cells. Lines had been carved into the east-side wall from pieces of cement that had cracked and fallen to the ground. The west-side wall had been covered in pictographs and random geometrical shapes to alleviate the boredom of solitude. There were moments throughout the day when a small stream of light would peek through the boarded-up window. It was just enough to confirm the sun still existed outside the prison walls.

The water on the floor started to ripple. Earthquakes were common, breaking up the mundane and monotonous time spent staring at the wall. The magnitude of this earthquake felt more intense than usual. The ceiling cracked, and shards of concrete flaked off and hit the ground. The doors rattled, and the sounds of water pipes bursting could be heard throughout the prison.

Some of the doors to the cells cracked open, and men ran in different directions. Some walked out of their cells only to fall down in the hall out of sheer starvation. Sirens were blaring, and guards ran for shelter, as they were in just as much fear for their lives as the prisoners.

A middle-aged man ran past the door just as a large beam fell, pinning him down against the newly made barricade. He reached out and cried for help but didn't see anyone around to help him. His arm went down, and he hung his head in defeat right before the beam was lifted off him and thrown to the side. Freed from the obstruction, the man looked up, and Carl reached down his hand toward his.

"Come on! This way!"

www.ingramcontent.com/pod-product-compliance
Lightning Source LLC
Chambersburg PA
CBHW051514150726
47997CB00001B/240